Colton Martinez is a seahorse shifter and lives a comfortable life at *World of Aquatica*, a shifter owned and operated marine park. When a number of others find their Fate-given mates, he doesn't give finding his own much thought—until he scents the most alluring aroma in a big, handsome human named Waylon Davison. Discovering his mate has a boy-friend doesn't deter Colton. Instead, he lifts Waylon's wallet and, with the help of friends, plans his strategy for wooing the man. After learning his human is disturbingly cowed by his boyfriend, Colton realizes Waylon has more to overcome than the shock of discovering that shifters exist. Even if Colton can convince Waylon to dump his jerk of a boyfriend, can he convince his human that entering a pairing with a man chosen by Fate isn't a new prison?

Surfing with a Seahorse
Copyright © 2019 Charlie Richards
ISBN: 978-1-4874-2650-7
Cover art by Angela Waters

Published by eXtasy Books Inc or
Devine Destinies, an imprint of eXtasy Books Inc

Look for us online at:
www.eXtasybooks.com or www.devinedestinies.com

SURFING WITH A SEAHORSE BENEATH AQUATICA'S WAVES: BOOK SIX

BY

CHARLIE RICHARDS

DEDICATION

And above all watch with glittering eyes the whole world around you because the greatest secrets are always hidden in the most unlikely places. Those who don't believe in magic will never find it.
Roald Dahl

CHAPTER ONE

In seahorse form, Colton slipped inside the man-made coral reef. He wrapped his prehensile tail around a hidden lever and used his minuscule weight to tug it down. A panel immediately opened beneath him.

Colton sank into the passageway. As soon as his tiny body tripped the sensor—which was damn near immediately—the panel above him slid closed. In the next instant, a water cycle began, and the current flushed him along the tube and into an underground pool. His small body swirled around while Colton found his bearings.

As soon as Colton recognized the sea-green tiles on the walls, he began to shift. His small body expanded. His bones and muscles popped and cracked as they rearranged under the surface of his skin. After so many years, he easily held his breath as his gills disappeared and his lungs formed.

Quickly getting control of his newly formed limbs, Colton kicked his legs and swished his arms. His head broke the surface. He sucked in a lungful of air.

Colton glanced around the underground pool area, taking in the space. The steps were just off to his left, so he started in that direction. He carefully maneuvered around other shifters, not wanting to disturb them as they went through their change.

He wasn't the only one coming off his shift, after all.

Almost ten years before, Colton had found his tiny seahorse trapped by the tentacle of a giant squid. To his shock, the beast hadn't eaten him. Instead, it had brought him to the surface just above the coral reef along the waters of Miami, and he'd shifted.

Then the dominant male had demanded that Colton shift, too.

While shocking, it had been the best thing to ever happen to Colton. After all, the huge shifter had offered him a way out of his piss-ant life as a street thief. The big, green-eyed male — who he'd learned was named William Roush — had offered him a home and a purpose.

World of Aquatica.

The place was a massive marine park. What humans didn't know, however, was that the facility was run by shifters who shared their spirits with aquatic and semi-aquatic animals. While some of the exhibits contained regular beasts, just about all of the larger, more exotic beasts — from dolphins to sharks to whales — were actually shifters.

It made putting on shows and offering exotic adventures much safer . . . and much more lucrative.

As a seahorse shifter, Colton didn't partake in all that. He hung out in a massive aquarium for several hours for a few days a week. The rest of his time was spent on what he was really good at — working on vehicles. As he strode up the pool's steps, he thought about the rest of his day.

Colton needed to fix a rock chip in one fellow shifter's windshield. That would only take a few minutes. The brake job on the —

"Oh, excuse me."

Pulled from his thoughts, Colton smiled and nodded at the woman who'd nearly slipped and bumped into him on the steps. He gripped her upper arm. "You okay, Sasha?" he asked, making certain she had her balance.

Rolling her eyes, Sasha nodded and pulled away. "Yep. You're not the only one lost in thought." She quickly hustled on her way.

Colton's gaze didn't even stray to her naked butt as he followed her into the unisex locker room. As a fellow shifter—Sasha shared her spirit with a sea turtle—nudity was a common thing amongst them all. Without giving it a second thought, Colton strode past a pair of naked men discussing the rest of their afternoon and stopped at his locker.

He opened the door and grabbed a towel. As he quickly dried himself, he recalled the last vehicle service job he had planned for that afternoon. He needed to get beneath the hood of the car owned by Beta William's mate—Captain John Casinov—and figure out what was causing his dashboard electrical items to go on the fritz. Sometimes the man would lose his horn, other times his radio, and more often than not, his air conditioner. The dash lights flashing off gave him a place to start, and he—

The rumbling of Colton's stomach caught his attention, and he snickered.

Definitely food first, though.

Shifting left Colton hungry on the best day. His body expended a lot of calories when it changed from a human form to a tiny seahorse . . . or vice versa. Since Colton had only grabbed a bagel for breakfast—he'd hit the snooze button one too many times because the prior evening he'd gotten sucked into a technical journal—he felt damn near starving.

Colton headed to *Mini Barrier Reef Cantina*, a nice restaurant in the marine park. His mouth watered for a big bowl of their steamer clams. After eating all the clams, he anticipated sopping up the delicious white wine sauce they came in with hunks of buttered bread.

His stomach rumbled again, and Colton picked up his pace.

When Colton arrived at the restaurant, he greeted Thane, who stood behind the podium. The man was usually a waiter, so he had to ask, "What are you doing up here?"

"Natalie wasn't feeling well, so she asked me to cover her

shift," Thane replied, a bright smile on the blond's face. Colton noticed it didn't quite meet his green eyes as it usually did, betraying his concern as easily as his scent did.

Colton patted Thane on the shoulder. "I hope it's nothing serious."

"Me, too," Thane replied. "I'm gonna take some soup to her after this shift to check on her." He quickly shifted gears, asking, "Table for one? Or are we expecting others?"

"Just me," Colton told him, patting his belly. "Need a quick lunch before heading to the shop."

Thane nodded as he grabbed a menu, then led the way through the restaurant. Placing the menu on a small table with two chairs, he offered, "Kayne will be here in a moment."

"Thanks, Thane." Colton knew the man referenced his brother, who also worked as a server there, and picked up the menu, even though he already knew what he wanted. "Wonder what the pie is today."

"Hey, Colton," Kayne greeted a moment later, arriving with a glass of water and a grin. "Want anything besides the water to drink? Want to hear the specials?"

Colton immediately picked up the water as he replied, "No need, and the water's good. Want the steamer clams. But what pie is available?" Then he drank half the glass.

Kayne nodded as he jotted the request on his order pad. At the same time, he told him, "There's peach pie, lemon meringue, or apple cobbler."

Humming appreciatively, Colton stated, "The cobbler." He grinned widely. "You know me so well."

Laughing, Kayne headed back toward the kitchen, pausing at various tables along the way.

Colton pulled out his phone and opened his reading app. Just as he began a technical journal, an interesting scent wafted over his nostrils. He lifted his head and inhaled deeply as he glanced around.

A large, black-skinned male strode past his table, and for just an instant, their eyes met. His deep-gray eyes widened as he perused Colton's body, then he looked away. He swallowed hard as he hurried on his way . . . taking the mouth-watering scent with him.

"Oh, fuck me," Colton whispered, turning and staring at the human's sexy ass, sadly hidden behind loose board shorts. He still found it a thing of beauty, and the desire to follow and proposition him in the bathroom surged through him.

Colton almost rose to do just that when he felt his seahorse trill in his mind.

Mate.

Freezing, Colton swallowed hard. His mouth went dry. He grabbed his water and took a deep swallow.

Holy shit. That's my mate? Damn, Fate knows me so well.

The human had pinged just about every one of his boxes. He had to have stood at least six-foot-three, maybe an inch more. His shoulders were wide, stretching his t-shirt, and his torso tapered to a trim waist. The muscles of his arms and calves bulged, giving the idea of an active lifestyle.

Realizing he was just sitting there when his mate was in the room, Colton rose to his feet and strode swiftly toward the hall where the restrooms were tucked. He turned the corner and ran into a wall of muscle. Huge hands gripped his upper arms, keeping him from landing on his ass.

"Damn, sorry about that, man," a deep voice laced with concern said. "Didn't expect ya." The hands disappeared, and the man took a step backward.

Yep, definitely six-foot-four. And gods, what a gorgeous deep voice.

Colton grinned up at the handsome man. "Not a problem. Just wanted to catch up with you."

"Me?" The man's black eyebrows furrowed. "Is something wrong?"

"What's going on?" A slender Caucasian human rounded Colton and stopped beside Colton's mate. He wrapped his arm around the human's waist possessively. When he lifted an imperious brow and stared brazenly at him, Colton wanted to deck him.

Well, at least I know he's openly gay.

Switching gears, Colton grinned widely. "Sorry, man. Just thought he was someone I know," he lied, waving at his mate. Although that was actually kinda true . . . after all, a shifter *knew* his mate by scent. He shrugged. "I was wrong." Holding out his hand to the man he hoped to soon steal, Colton offered, "I'm Colton Martinez. Sorry for the confusion."

"Waylon Davison," the huge man replied, taking Colton's hand. His nostrils flared, and his eyes widened just a little, betraying that he too felt the connection. Still holding Colton's hand, Waylon used the other to indicate the Caucasian. "This is my boyfriend, Richard Leander."

Nodding, Colton managed to release Waylon even though he would much rather have preferred to use the hold to pull his mate away from Richard. "Well, I work here, so if you have any questions, just holler." He began sidling around Waylon, keeping a smile on his face as he glanced between them, making certain both men's focus remained on his face. "I'll be back at my table eating lunch in just a minute."

Then, using skills he hadn't had to utilize in over a decade—since before his time as the marine park's mechanic—Colton easily lifted Waylon's wallet.

Waylon Davison couldn't take his eyes off Colton's ass until the man disappeared into the men's room.

"God, you could at least be a little more subtle when you're eye-fucking another man. I *am* standing right here."

Upon hearing Richard's snide, angrily-hissed words, Waylon fought back a wince. His boyfriend was right, unfortunately. He should have been more careful . . . or maybe not done it at all.

Especially since Richard's so jealous and already in a bad mood.

Slinging his arm around Richard's shoulders, Waylon forced a smile as he met his boyfriend's gaze. "Sorry, Richie. It wasn't really what you thought," he hedged, hoping to avoid a lecture. Waylon started them back to their table. "I was just trying to see if he jogged my memory. He said he thought we knew each other." Waylon shrugged, grinning. "But it seems he was wrong."

"Of course he was wrong," Richard replied hotly. "And come on. I already paid. Let's go to the underwater aquarium."

"Sounds good." Waylon didn't care where they went as long as it shifted Richard's focus.

As soon as they left the restaurant, however, Waylon realized he wasn't that lucky.

Turning to the left, Richard took Waylon's hand possessively. "And that guy was totally lying. I saw him staring at your ass when you passed his table," Richard stated, frowning. "That's why I came over."

Waylon nodded, deciding to simply say, "Oh."

What else could he say? He sure as hell couldn't tell Richard that the man's attention had been flattering. The Hispanic man had been damn pretty with his olive-skinned features, short black hair, and sparkling dark-brown eyes. His wide smile had held appreciation as he swept his gaze up and down Waylon's body when he'd walked by his table.

Yeah, I noticed him, too.

Waylon had needed to think unsexy thoughts in order to get his plumping dick to soften so he could relieve his aching bladder. Then when he'd bumped into him, the feel of his strong shoulders under his palms and the guy's lithe body against his own had sent arousal sizzling through him. He'd had to back up a step and release him, so he didn't sprout wood in a big way.

That would have been very bad, because Richard would have noticed, and he would have gotten an earful for another reason.

It wasn't my fault that a school field trip made it so we couldn't see the morning tiger shark exhibit.

"Oh? That's all you're going to say?"

Waylon sighed as he squeezed Richard's hand. "What do you want me to say, Richie?" He tried to sound soothing. "You're my boyfriend. Not him. I'm leaving here with you."

They'd been dating for almost six months, and in that time, Richard enjoyed saying the possessive statement to him. Waylon hoped it helped coming from his own mouth. He didn't know how else to convince the man.

At this point, Waylon barely even saw his friends anymore. Richard always wanted to hang out, and he made excuses as to why they shouldn't invite Waylon's buddies to join them. Waylon knew something would have to give soon, because he was damn tired of stroking Richard's ego.

But he sucks like a hoover and has an ass to die for.

Waylon's prick began to plump a bit as he recalled the way Richard had bounced on his cock the prior evening.

Unfortunately, in an instant, the image of a certain Hispanic man super-imposed itself on his memory.

Shit.

Pushing away his thoughts, Waylon focused on what he should be . . . his date with Richard.

After spending hours at *World of Aquatica*, Waylon strolled through the parking lot toward his truck. He pushed the unlock button on his key fob as he arrived at the passenger door. Opening it for Richard, he leaned down and gave him a perfunctory kiss.

Waylon rounded the hood, suddenly feeling odd . . . uncomfortable even. Glancing around, he tried to spot anyone watching, but no one seemed to be paying him any mind. He opened his door and climbed in, trying to dismiss the sensation.

"Everything okay?" Richard asked, cocking his head.

"Mmm-hmm," Waylon said with a nod. He flashed a smile Richard's way as he shoved the key into the slot. "Are you hungry?" It had been hours since lunch. "Did you want to pick up something on the way to your place?"

Waylon put his truck into gear and started them on their way.

"Well, I thought we could go to your apartment, Wayway," Richard countered, his tone seductive. He reached over the bench seat and rested his hand on Waylon's shoulder. As Richard teased his fingertips up and down the line of his neck, he continued to purr, "We can order in and curl up together. Put in a movie that we won't watch."

As much as Waylon hated that nickname, he couldn't bring himself to say anything about it. Richard only used it when attempting to arouse him. Normally, what he was doing would have done it, too.

Waylon loved having his neck touched and the skin over his tendons teased.

Unfortunately, for some reason, Waylon felt the urge to move away from Richard. He resisted, but he couldn't bring himself to agree either. Instead, something sour curdled his stomach, making him feel a little queasy.

What the hell?

Rubbing at his stomach, Waylon muttered, "You know, I'm real sorry, Richie, but I'm not really feeling so hot." He gave Richard a side-eyed glance as he told him, "If it's okay with you, I'm just gonna drop you off and go home."

Richard scowled, straightening. "Seriously?"

Waylon had never turned down sex with Richard. He

loved sex—always had. They'd even fucked when he had a fever once because Richard had worked him up. Waylon realized turning down his boyfriend had to be a red flag to him.

"I'm sorry," Waylon repeated even as he nodded. "I just—" He sighed and rubbed the back of his neck. "I don't feel well, and if I'm late to work or miss one more day, my boss is gonna fire me."

The man had threatened it enough.

Asshole.

Huffing a sigh, Richard crossed his arms over his chest. "Fine, but I want roses when you come over Monday evening, or I'm not putting out."

Waylon reached over and squeezed Richard's thigh. "Sure, Richie."

Just that fast, Waylon's stomach began to settle.

Weird.

Chapter Two

Colton strode into the security office. Spotting the guard behind the reception desk, he asked, "Is Ovram in his office?"

Mason, the guard, nodded. The bull shark shifter cocked his head. "Want me to call him?"

Already moving past Mason, Colton shook his head. "Naw. I need his help with computer shit, so I'll go there."

"All right."

Moving swiftly, Colton soon stood outside Ovram's office door. He knocked once but didn't bother waiting for a response. Too eager, he let himself in.

Ovram was just turning in his chair, and upon spotting him, the sea lion shifter's brows shot up. "Colton. Hey. What's up?"

Pulling out the pilfered wallet, Colton handed over Waylon's driver's license. "I need a background check on this man."

Taking the license, Ovram began turning back to his desk. "Do I *want* to know why you have Waylon's wallet?" He smirked over his shoulder, then began typing. "Am I just confirming the address? Or do you really want a background check?"

"Really a background check, and I have his wallet because I stole it."

Ovram barked a laugh. "What? Why?"

"He's my mate."

Whipping back around, Ovram gaped at him. "Your mate?

Damn! That's fantastic." He bounced up from his seat and gave Colton a quick hug. Returning to his chair, he began to type swiftly. "So where is he? Got him stashed in your room already?" Ovram cast a sly look Colton's way.

Colton sighed deeply, crossing his arms over his chest as he leaned against Ovram's desk. "Afraid not. He was here with his boyfriend."

"His boyfriend?" Ovram parroted. "Well, that's shit luck, huh?"

"Eh, at least I know he's out." Colton decided to think positively. "I need to know where he works. Hobbies. Friends. Shit like that. That way, I can begin fitting my way into his life, so I can steal him."

"Don't you mean woo him?" Chortling, Ovram continued dancing his fingers over the keys.

Colton shoved his hands into his pockets and shrugged. "Sure. That, too."

Ovram glanced his way again, his expression sobering. "Have you told the alpha, yet?"

"Hmmm," Colton mused as he pulled out his phone. "Probably a good idea."

With the discovery of his mate, Colton could admit he'd been a little overwhelmed. His thoughts had been consumed with figuring out how to extricate him from the possessive boyfriend. He hadn't thought beyond that.

Dialing Alpha Kaiser's number, Colton lifted the phone to his ear and waited. The alpha and his younger brother, William, were the leaders of their pod. They handled the tough decisions, such as overseeing the safety of all the shifters under their care and dealing with outsiders as well as the general running of the park.

Colton appreciated that, for the most part, he was left alone to work on the cars.

Cars. Right. Gotta get to that, too.

Just because he'd found his mate didn't mean he could

shirk all his responsibilities.

"Colton, what can I help you with?"

Hearing Alpha Kaiser's voice drew Colton back to what he was doing. "I found my mate, Alpha Kaiser. I thought I should let you know," he stated bluntly.

"Really?" Kaiser's tone registered surprise. "When? Where? Do you know yet if you're going to need help wooing him? Where are you? It'll be easier to discuss in person."

Colton smiled upon hearing Kaiser's barrage of questions. That was definitely something he appreciated—the quick attention and care of the alpha and beta brothers. Not having grown up in a pod when younger, Colton had found it an amazing change.

"I'm at the security office with Ovram, Alpha," Colton told him. "I ran into Waylon in *Mini Barrier Reef Cantina*, and since his boyfriend interrupted me introducing myself to him and scented of possessive jealousy, I headed off, but not before lifting his wallet. Ovram is pulling information on him now."

Kaiser laughed, the sound deep and rich. "I'll be right there," he got out between chuckles, then the line disconnected.

"The alpha sure got a kick out of that," Ovram commented as he drew Colton's attention to his screen. "Your man's a bartender and waiter at a chain restaurant in town. *Scooter's Bar and Grill*."

Reading the information on the screen, Colton absently stated, "The alpha probably thought it was so funny because I lifted Beta William's wallet when I first met them. I was a right good thief back in the day."

"You stole Beta William's wallet?" Ovram asked, gasping. "When? Why? Did they catch you?"

Colton replied, "Because I was a thief by necessity. I didn't have any identification since as a seahorse shifter, I was born in my animal form. And, yeah, they caught me. I'm here, aren't I?" Snorting, he muttered, "Thought I was gonna be eaten by a squid." He pointed at the screen. "He enjoys surfing." Straightening, Colton grinned. "Sweet."

"Wait. You were born in your animal form?" Ovram cocked his head, scowling. "I didn't think that was possible."

"It's rare," Alpha Kaiser stated, striding into the room. "Happening only in a few aquatic species." He reached out and gripped Colton's shoulder, giving it a light squeeze as he smiled at him. "Congratulations."

"Thank you, Alpha Kaiser," Colton responded. "I'd like to request the use of the south cliff beach."

Alpha Kaiser nodded, a smirk curving his lips as he peered at the screen. "That big man is a surfer? He must have impressive balance." Releasing Colton, he added, "I'll spread the word. Now . . . you said he has a boyfriend? How big of a problem do you think he'll be?"

Colton curled his lip as he thought about Richard. "He was possessive. Not sure how long they've been together. I'll let you know once I learn more."

"Good. Good." Kaiser opened his mouth to say more, but he paused when his brother William breezed into the room.

William grabbed Colton and hugged him. "Congrats, man. I just heard the good news!"

"How?" Colton couldn't help but ask.

William laughed, pointing over his shoulder. "You left Ovram's door open, and Eban is sitting in his office. He sent out a text to the inner circle."

Colton nodded, understanding. Eban was the pod's head enforcer, so he took security very seriously.

"So, tell me about him," William ordered, propping his ass on the side of Ovram's desk.

For the third time in fifteen minutes, Colton shared what little he knew about Waylon.

Groaning, Waylon wanted to bash his head against the wall. He didn't know how it had happened, but he couldn't find his wallet. He'd noticed it missing when he'd planned to order a pizza. He'd already searched his pick-up and feared he'd lost it at *World of Aquatica*.

Just great.

Waylon pulled a file out of his desk and began leafing through the pages. "I know my bank and credit card shit are in here somewhere." Seeing as he struggled with computers enough, he decided doing an online search would be a last resort.

"Ah, here's my bank's number, at least," Waylon mumbled. Just as he began dialing the eight hundred number to report a lost or stolen card, his doorbell rang.

Shoving his phone back into his pocket, Waylon crossed to the door. He peered through the peephole. Upon spotting who stood on the other side, he felt his gut clench.

How the hell?

Waylon heard the doorbell again. After counting to five and taking a couple of long breaths, he opened it and stared at the man. The stranger he'd bumped into at the restaurant was just as stunning as the first time he'd seen him.

"Yes?" Waylon asked warily.

How had the man—Colton, if he remembered correctly— found his home?

Colton grinned broadly, his dark eyes gleaming. "Hey, Waylon. Nice to see you again." His focus slid down Waylon's frame, then back up, the appreciation in his expression clear. "A lot of you."

Waylon knew if his skin hadn't been so dark, he would be blushing. Still, his cheeks heated, and his mouth went dry. Rubbing absently at his bare chest, he tried to figure out what to say.

After Waylon had dropped off Richard, he'd returned

home and changed into a comfortable pair of cut-off sweat shorts . . . and that was it.

"Can I come in for a minute?" Colton took a step forward, invading Waylon's space brazenly. "I won't be but a minute, if you don't want me to be."

What Waylon wanted Colton to do to him flashed through his mind, but he shook it off. *I'm in a relationship, and I'm no cheater.* In the past, Waylon had never even been tempted, but as he took a couple of steps backward to allow Colton to pass, his blood heated as he took in the much smaller man's confident swagger.

The form-fitting jeans and t-shirt Colton wore left very little to the imagination, and Waylon's fingers twitched with an unexpected urge to touch.

"Thanks, hottie," Colton stated, stopping in the living room of Waylon's one-bedroom apartment. His gaze fell on Waylon's surfboard where it rested against the far wall. Grinning widely, Colton crossed to it. "Nice board, Way." He ran his palm down the side appreciatively. "High end." Spinning, he peered at him, palms out. "I gotta show you this private stretch owned by Aquatica. Amazing waves pretty much all the time." Colton shrugged, a chuckle entering his tone. "Well, unless there's a storm. Then watch out!"

Waylon opened his mouth, then closed it again. *Damn, this guy can talk.* It caused a smile to curve his lips because he found he liked the tenor timbre of Colton's voice. *Not what I'm supposed to be focusing on.* Closing the door, he drew nearer the tempting man.

Except, instead of asking why Colton was there, something else came out.

"Yeah, I like to surf," Waylon admitted. He didn't get to do it nearly as often as he liked since he'd hooked up with Richard. The friends he normally surfed with were the ones his boyfriend didn't get along with. "I know most of the beaches around here. What one do you mean?"

"It's a private one on property owned by *World of Aquatica*," Colton told him, grinning widely. "But as an employee, I have access to it." He rubbed his palm over the board again. "Come with me. You'll be able to really put this baby through its paces."

God, it's so damn tempting.

Except, Waylon didn't know this man.

"How did you find me?" Waylon narrowed his eyes and crossed his arms over his chest. He would never actually hurt the man, but he needed answers.

"Oh, with this." Colton pulled out Waylon's missing wallet and held it out. "I found it on the bench seat of your table. It must have fallen out of your pocket." When Waylon took it, Colton rested his hand on his wrist, squeezing lightly. "I looked for you, but your boyfriend had already hustled you away. He's a little"—he hummed for a second before finishing—"intense."

Waylon figured that wasn't the word Colton had originally planned to use. Even as he opened his mouth to defend his lover, his voice stalled. Instead, Waylon found his focus drifting to where Colton held his wrist.

Colton gently rubbed the pad of his thumb over Waylon's pulse point in a light, rhythmic massage. The hairs on his arm stood on end. Goose bumps rose on his flesh. Even his nipples beaded.

Holy shit!

Clearing his throat, Waylon pulled away, breaking the contact. Immediately, he wanted to feel those sensations again. His heart hammered in his chest, and he knew that spending too much time in Colton's company could spell trouble.

"Th-Thank you for returning this," Waylon said, holding up his wallet. He took a few steps away, using the action of setting it on the end table to put some distance between them. Clearing his throat, Waylon rubbed the back of his neck. "I just realized it was missing half an hour ago."

"I was gonna try tracking you down in the park, but it's a big park," Colton told him with a laugh. "Plus, I had to get to work."

"Oh? Where do you work?"

Why am I extending his stay by asking about him?

Colton grinned, clearly pleased. "I'm a mechanic. I work on the vehicles of the employees of the park. One of the perks of working there. Free auto repair," he explained with a dismissive roll of his shoulder. "What about you?"

"I work at *Scooter's Bar and Grill* at their bar. I also tend the tables in that area."

To Waylon's surprise, he felt his cheeks heat once more. He'd never been embarrassed of his job before, but he figured working on vehicles took all kinds of certifications and training. Colton must have had plenty of schooling.

"Yeah? Never been to one." Colton sidled closer again. "Is their food good?"

Waylon nodded. "They have some amazing southwestern egg rolls, and a chocolate lava cake that—" He hummed as he rubbed his belly. "Can't eat that too often, but damn."

Colton laughed as he eyed where Waylon rubbed his stomach. "Looks like you could handle a few just fine." When he returned his focus to Waylon's eyes, his gaze smoldered. "Especially if you join me surfing. I'll help you work it off."

A shiver worked up Waylon's spine as arousal zinged through him. His balls churned, and his cock thickened. He knew if he looked down, he would be tenting his cut-offs.

As tempting as it was to lower his hand and cover himself, Waylon knew that would just draw more attention to his predicament. Instead, he cleared his throat before mumbling, "You know I have a boyfriend."

"I know." Colton's dark eyes narrowed. His nostrils flared, and he peered pointedly at Waylon's crotch before meeting his gaze. A hungry smile curved his lips. "I also know the chemistry between us is electric."

Waylon couldn't deny that. Still, he shook his head. "I won't cheat," he rumbled gruffly. "I can't go on a date with you."

Colton stepped even closer and rested his palm on Waylon's chest. "While I'd love to call it a date, I understand."

Rubbing lightly, Colton skimmed his thumb over Waylon's nipple, causing a zing to shoot through his torso.

Waylon swallowed hard as his nipple throbbed pleasantly.

"This will be two guys hangin' out and surfing. Just having a good time." His expression turned sultry. "That way, we'll already know each other when you're ready to accept what's happening between us."

"What's happening between us?" Waylon asked breathlessly.

Colton chuckled roughly as he took a step backward, severing the contact. Pulling a sheet of paper from his back pocket, he handed it over. "This is my phone number and where and when to meet me with your board tomorrow, Waylon."

Waylon took it on reflex.

As Colton passed him, heading toward the door, he brushed his hand down Waylon's side. Then he crossed to the door and opened it. Pausing on the threshold, he purred, "And Waylon, we're connecting."

Rubbing his chest as the door closed, Waylon felt as if his heart had skipped a beat.

What the hell just happened here?

Even though Waylon knew he should just throw the paper away, he couldn't bring himself to do it.

CHAPTER THREE

"Think he'll show?"

Colton turned and eyed Enforcer Westram. The longnosed sawshark shifter had been assigned to watch the beach while an unknowing human surfed in the area. Of course, Waylon wouldn't know he was there, since as soon as he arrived, Westram would dive into the sea and turn into his animal.

In that form, Westram would make certain no other shifters tried to utilize the beach. Even though messages had been sent out to everyone in the pod, someone might have missed it. Alpha Kaiser had thought it best to overcome one hurdle at a time.

Colton had silently agreed and had appreciated the aid of his friends.

"I'm not certain," Colton admitted, resting some of his weight against the gate that kept the general public out of the area. His vehicle was parked just beyond it, his board strapped to the roof.

Westram straddled a dirt bike, ready to take off . . . if Waylon actually showed up.

"What'll you try next if he doesn't?"

Sighing, Colton cocked his head. "Drop by his work." He grinned and waggled his brows at his friend. "I'll probably do it anyway."

"Well, while you're surfing, Ovram will put a trace on his phone." Westram grinned. "That way we can—" He paused, his eyes narrowing.

Colton turned, hearing what Westram did. A vehicle approached. He grinned, chuckling low in his throat.

"Seems I got to him after all," Colton rumbled, pleasure flooding him. Then he laughed. "Either that or it was the allure of surfing a new area."

Westram patted his shoulder. "Never under-estimate the mate-pull." Then he fired up the dirt bike and took off.

Colton remained leaning against the gate, waiting for the vehicle to appear. When it did, his heart rate sped up. The older *Dodge* pick-up appeared in decent shape, but Colton could hear a couple of things slightly off.

His fingers twitched with his desire to get under the hood.

Another time, he promised himself.

When the truck pulled to a stop behind Colton's *Wrangler*, Colton pushed off the gate and swung it closed, but he didn't relock it.

"Hi, Colton."

Upon hearing his mate's deep voice, Colton inhaled, deep and slow. *Gods, he sounds good.* As much as he wanted to use every second of their not-date seducing his human, Colton wouldn't go back on his word.

No touching.

That didn't mean he couldn't provoke a response in other ways. After all, he knew he looked damn fine in the wetsuit he used for surfing. He imagined Waylon would look fantastic, too.

Gods, my dick is going to be strangled today.

Colton figured he should have thought about that before, but it was too late now. "Hi, Waylon," he said, turning and grinning at the big, black man. He swept his gaze over his mate, taking in the navy green tank top and dark-blue board shorts. The sandals he wore on his big feet showed off neatly trimmed toenails. "Shit. Even his feet are sexy."

"What?" Waylon's black brows furrowed, and he rubbed his hand over his bald head. He glanced down. "What about my feet?"

Realizing he'd been overheard, Colton barked a laugh as he crossed to him. "Just admiring them." He patted the big man's upper arm. "Come on, Waylon. Follow me down the trail. Glad you got a truck. The way is rocky."

Waylon nodded almost absently, as if he were trying to figure out if Colton was telling him the truth.

Colton didn't care for that response, but he didn't say anything about it. Instead, he climbed into his *Jeep* and began the slow trek down the rutted lane. Keeping an eye on the rearview mirror, Colton saw Waylon's truck had little difficulty.

Good.

Reaching a slightly sloped clearing, Colton parked and hopped out. He waved and pointed, indicating where his human should park. Then he began pulling his board free of the rack.

After Colton rested it against the back of his *Wrangler*, he pulled out his wetsuit. Without hesitation, he stripped, keeping his back toward the truck.

"Holy shit."

Colton heard Waylon's hissed words and grinned. Peering over his shoulder, he spotted Waylon standing at the foot of his truck. His eyes were wide, and he was ogling Colton's ass.

Chuckling huskily, Colton purred, "Sorry, Way. Forgot most people don't go commando." Picking up the speedo that had been tucked between the folds of the wetsuit, he added loudly, "But even I won't wear a wetsuit against my cock and balls."

Then Colton bent, and while flexing his ass cheeks, he stepped into the small bathing suit. After pulling it up his legs and settling it in place, he turned around to face his mate. Colton brazenly adjusted his half-hard shaft as he eyed the other man.

Waylon hadn't moved from his position at the foot of his truck . . . but now his shorts were blatantly tented. His hands were at his sides, and his fingers twitched. The way his chest heaved and how his lips were parted betrayed his need.

On top of that, Colton caught the earthy fragrance of Waylon's lust.

Delicious.

"Waylon?" Colton called his name softly, causing the other man to blink. He jerked his attention upward, meeting his gaze. Seeing the internal struggle going on behind his mate's eyes, Colton decided he'd teased enough for now. He didn't want his human doing something he would feel guilty about later. "Waylon? Gonna get dressed?"

After blinking once, twice, a shudder worked through Waylon's body.

Colton loved that response. Too bad he couldn't do anything about it. Instead, he knew he needed to give the man a chance to regain his dignity.

To that end, Colton began easing into his wetsuit. After a few more seconds, Waylon started to do the same.

Once they were both ready with their boards tucked under their arms, Colton led the way down a set of stone steps carved into the side of the cliff. "Watch your step," he advised. Glancing behind him, he caught the spike of unease in his mate's scent. "Damn. I should have asked if you're okay with heights."

"Not exactly a fan. No," Waylon admitted, staying as close to the face of the cliff as possible. "Maybe it comes from being so tall."

Colton recognized an attempt at mirth. "Maybe." Hoping to distract him, he asked, "Tell me about your truck. Have you had it long?" He grinned over his shoulder at him. "I'm a mechanic. I heard a few things."

That seemed to do the trick.

As they walked to the beach, Waylon began sharing about his truck. The way he spoke of the seventy-two *Dodge* pick-up betrayed the love he had for the vehicle. He explained how when he'd bought it at auction, the thing barely ran. Over the course of the four years he'd had it, he'd dumped a shitload of time, energy, and money into getting it looking and running as well as it did.

"Are you opposed to anyone else looking at her?" Colton asked as he placed his towel and satchel — which contained his phone, a few snacks for later, and a small first aid kit — onto a rock near the edge of the beach. Colton waggled his brows. "I *am* a mechanic, after all."

Waylon set his own towel and bag down, then hefted his board. "I'm not against it. Just never had the cash to have a professional give her a peek," he admitted, rubbing the back of his neck.

Colton had realized quickly enough that Waylon did that when he was uncomfortable or uncertain. Wanting the man at ease with him, he laughed brightly. "Well, good thing we're friends now, aren't we?" Giving Waylon's impressive bicep a squeeze — *yum* — he added, "Come on, man. These waves look killer."

Then Colton started down the beach.

For the next hour and a half, Colton paddled, waited for the right second, then leaped onto his board. He rode the waves, skimming along the surface of the water. Relishing the salty spray and the fresh ocean scent, Colton kept an eye on the man he hoped would soon turn into his lover and partner in life.

Spotting how Waylon's movements began to grow sluggish, Colton rode the waves toward shore. He beckoned the other man, urging him to follow. Seeing Waylon's nod, he finished his glide to the beach and carried his board toward where they'd left his stuff.

Colton rested his board carefully against a large rock. Then he unzipped his suit partway down, pushing it down to his waist. As much as he would love to remove it entirely, Colton didn't want to push Waylon too far out of his comfort zone.

When Waylon joined him, Colton grinned up at him. "Hey, time for a break and a snack," he urged, waving toward a rock as he used his towel to wipe over his head and face. "Have a seat."

At first, Waylon appeared uncertain, but he obeyed.

Nice.

Waylon tried not to stare at the smooth olive skin of Colton's chest. He did his best not to notice the dusky areola or the way his peach nipples were budded. His mouth did not water at the sight of the ridge straining against Colton's groin.

As Waylon settled on a nearby rock and rubbed himself with his towel, he attempted to ignore his own throbbing shaft. He couldn't remember the last time he'd been so hard for so long. Spending time with Colton was the most painful and thrilling couple of hours of his life.

"Nothing fancy," Colton claimed as he pulled out a thermal lunch sack from his knapsack. "Roasted sunflower seeds, peanuts, slices of pepperjack cheese."

As Colton said each item, he set it on a cloth napkin he'd placed on a rock between them. The man had planned ahead. Just as he placed a package of pepperoni on the rock, he glanced up with a worried expression on his face.

"You're not allergic to anything. Are you?"

Waylon grinned as he shook his head. "Naw. I admit I don't eat a lot of gluten, but that's by choice."

Colton nodded as he pulled out another item. "Then you may want to steer clear of the peanut butter topped crackers." Then while placing a container of sliced vegetables on the napkin, he added, "Or you're welcome to use some of the veggies to scrape off the peanut butter and toss the crackers into the sea. Something's likely to enjoy that."

"I don't want to offend," Waylon responded slowly, reaching for a slice of cheese. "I mean, you went to the trouble of putting all this together."

Food hadn't even occurred to him. Although, he hadn't had much time after getting home from work. He'd thrown on some clothes before taking his stuff out to his truck.

Laughing, Colton shook his head. His brown eyes twinkling merrily. "You won't offend me." He waved his hand dismissively. "This is just so we don't die of starvation while resting our muscles to see if we have another round of energy for more surfing."

Even as Waylon nodded, he wondered if Colton was telling the truth. Anytime Richard cooked, it was always loaded with gluten—garlic bread, pasta, sandwiches, tacos with flour tortillas. While his boyfriend had assured him that he could eat any or all parts of the meal, Waylon had seen the way Richard would narrow his eyes with displeasure if he skipped certain parts.

Waylon felt as if he were walking through a minefield any time the man offered to prepare a meal.

"Whatever you're thinking about, knock it off, man," Colton ordered, his tone good-natured. "I say what I mean, and I don't normally lie."

"You said this wasn't a date, but you made food," Waylon blurted out. He grabbed a cucumber slice and shoved it in his mouth to keep himself from saying more.

It sure feels like a date.

Colton took a carrot stick and slid it through the peanut butter on one of the crackers, scraping nearly all of it off. Tossing the cracker into the sea, he held the carrot in his other hand. "I would love to go on a date with you, Waylon. I've never said otherwise, but this isn't a date." He waved his free hand at the ocean. "This is just a couple of guys hangin' out and doing something they both enjoy. Kinda like if we met up at a bar and played pool." Colton shrugged, then ate the peanut butter coated carrot stick.

Waylon took Colton at his word. "Okay." Then he grabbed a slice of cucumber, placed some pepperoni on top, before adding a bit of cheese. He popped everything into his mouth and hummed appreciatively, enjoying the flavors of the tasty morsel. As Waylon prepared another one, he asked, "So other than surfing, what do you do for fun?"

Chuckling, Colton admitted, "I'm pretty boring. I'm a homebody. I sit around and read technical journals about car manufacturing. Latest developments and releases and shit." Then he waggled his brows. "Of course, if I had someone to spend time with, I could be convinced to do other things. Dinner and a movie. Amusement parks. Hiking. Romantic picnics under a full moon."

"You're about as subtle as a wrecking ball," Waylon muttered around his mouthful of food. The cucumbers were crisp, the pepperoni flavorful, and the cheese spicy and sharp. Still, he couldn't help but smile.

Colton shrugged, clearly unrepentant. "I'm not going to lie. I told you that." His smile turned wry. "Just sitting here near you gets me hard, and I know I'm not the only one." Sliding his focus over Waylon's crotch, a hint of heat filled his eyes as he regarded him. "I bet I could make you damn happy."

"I bet you could, too," Waylon whispered, his gut clenching with his arousal. "I—"

The muffled sound of his phone drew his attention.

Waylon put his food down before rooting around in his bag and pulling out his phone. Seeing the number of missed calls, messages, and texts he had, he winced. The fact that Richard was calling for what looked like the sixth time just that evening didn't bode well.

Biting back a sigh, Waylon accepted the call. "Hi, Richie."

"Where the fuck are you?"

Hunching his shoulders, Waylon groaned mentally. "I'm surfing." As soon as the words were out of his mouth, he knew it had been the wrong thing to say. Unfortunately, just like Colton, Waylon wasn't a liar.

"I went by the beach, and you weren't there, so try again," Richard stated boldly, obviously thinking nothing of it that he'd just admitted to attempting to track him down. "Where are you?"

Waylon rubbed the back of his neck, uneasiness flooding him. "I'm at a new place. A friend showed it to me. The waves are epic. Wanna hear 'em?"

Maybe that would help.

"No, I don't want to hear them," Richard replied snidely. "I want to know why my boyfriend isn't here bringing me flowers like he said he would."

In point of fact, Waylon hadn't ever said that. Richard had ordered him to bring flowers the next time they got together. Of course, recalling the conversation, Waylon remembered that Richard had said to bring them that evening.

Shit.

"I'm sorry, babe," Waylon told him honestly. He was sorry . . . sorry his surfing was interrupted. "I'll be there as soon as I can."

"You better be." Then Richard disconnected the call.

Waylon rose and gathered his things. "I'm sorry," he repeated, forcing a smile. "I forgot that Richie was expecting me this evening, so I gotta cut this short." With a wave, Waylon began striding swiftly toward the stairs. "See you round."

"Yes, you will."

For some reason, Waylon hoped he hadn't imagined Colton's words.

CHAPTER FOUR

Colton stood before the mirror, checking his appearance.

"You ready?" Westram called before sticking his head into his bedroom. "Or you gonna stand in front of that mirror all day like a prima donna?"

"Ha, ha," Colton grumbled, turning away and heading toward the other shifter.

While Colton didn't know Westram exceedingly well, he appreciated the other male's support. After Waylon had run out on him two days before, he'd buried himself in work the next day. His seahorse had trilled quietly in his mind, and he had to agree.

One nasty phone call from the boyfriend and Waylon had gone running. As a shifter, he'd had no trouble hearing both sides of the conversation. What had really stabbed him through the heart was the mixture of annoyance, disappointment, and guilt that had been emanating from Waylon.

His mate hadn't wanted to leave him.

But he had.

That morning, Westram had shown up in the garage and smacked Colton upside the head. Then he'd reminded him that nothing good came easy. Westram had also presented him with Waylon's work schedule.

Suddenly, Colton had been so ready for a beer and some eggrolls.

"I'm ready," Colton stated, sounding calmer than he felt.

"Then let's roll." Westram patted him on the back, then led

the way out of his apartment. "I'm ready for a bacon cheese-burger with the works and a good beer."

Colton smiled. "That actually sounds really good, too." After his mate had ditched him, he hadn't had much of an appetite.

Westram grinned widely at him as he paused so Colton could lock his door. Winking, he started toward the stairs as he called, "And just think, the more you eat and the longer we take to enjoy it, the more time you'll have with your mate."

Processing that, Colton grinned widely. "Damn. I'm suddenly feeling ravenous."

Westram laughed some more.

"You ever been to this place?" Westram asked from where he sat in the passenger seat of Colton's *Wrangler*. "'Cause I haven't."

Colton parked in the lot as he shook his head. "No, but Waylon said the food was good." Then he turned off the engine and climbed from his vehicle.

"Cool. Let's feast."

Westram fell into step beside Colton, and the pair made their way to the front. The enforcer reached past him and opened the door. Colton strode inside, grabbed the second set of doors, and it was his turn to hold them open.

A second later, the hostess greeted them. "Welcome to *Scooter's Bar and Grill*." The blonde smiled widely as she glanced between them. "Table for two?"

Colton nodded even as he pointed toward the bar area, which was set apart to the left side. "You mind if we enjoy your bar area?"

"Feel free to sit anywhere you like," she told them, sweeping her arm in welcome.

Leading the way, Colton chose a booth directly to the left of the bar. It was close enough to be able to talk to Waylon if they chose, but not so near the man as to be intrusive. He didn't want to cause an issue with his job, after all.

As Westram slid onto the booth seat opposite him, the hostess placed their menus before them. "Waylon is manning the bar area this afternoon," she told them, still smiling as she glanced between them. "He'll be right out, I'm sure."

"Thank you," Colton replied.

As she walked away, Colton noticed that one booth on the opposite side of the bar area as well as one of the high-rise tables were also occupied. Since the area behind the bar was empty, he figured his mate was somewhere in back getting something for the other patrons. His assumption was proved correct when Waylon walked into the room carrying a platter of food.

Upon spotting them, Waylon froze, and his lips parted in obvious surprise.

Colton just smiled and nodded, then turned his attention back to the menu. A few moments later, Waylon arrived. He glanced between Colton and Westram while going through his spiel.

"Hey, Waylon," Colton rumbled softly, sweeping his gaze up and down the man appreciatively. While the black slacks and red button-down didn't show off his physique nearly as nicely as the tank tops and shorts, he still found the man stunning. "I figured I'd give the place a shot, since you gave it such a glowing review."

Waylon glanced at Westram again, and when his focus returned to Colton, his smile definitely appeared forced. "That's great. I hope you end up enjoying everything."

Guessing at what Waylon could be thinking didn't take much more than a sniff of the human's scent. Jealousy perfumed the air.

How about that?

"I'm very certain I will." Colton leaned toward Waylon, whispering, "Especially the service." Watching his mate's brows lift, he waved toward the other shifter. "This is Westram, a friend I've known for almost a decade." Colton lowered his voice further and told him, "This is also *not* a date."

To Colton's pleasure, the tightness of Waylon's shoulders eased, and the acrid tinge to his scent diminished.

Good.

Waylon nodded once, clearly flustered, even as he mumbled, "Well, um, okay. I—" Then he straightened and offered, "Can I start you with some drinks or an appetizer?"

"Both, please. Can we get some of those southwestern eggrolls you recommended? They sound good." Colton read through the alcohol menu. As he did that, Westram ordered a *Guinness* that was on tap. Humming, Colton mused, "That does sound good, but how about a *Michelob* amber."

"And waters, please," Westram piped up.

Colton nodded.

"I'll get that appetizer started, then build your beers," Waylon told them before turning away.

Still, Colton noticed the smile curving the man's lips and the pleasure filling his scent.

"It seems he's happy to see you, even if he is at work," Westram commented quietly, even as he reviewed the menu. He cast a wicked grin Colton's way before adding, "Maybe he has a break coming up, and you all can chat over his break while I drink a beer at the bar."

"Gods, that would be amazing." Colton sobered, grimacing. "You wouldn't mind?"

Westram chuckled, shaking his head. "Naw, I'll watch TV or read on my phone."

"Damn. Thanks."

"Anything to help a friend's *connection*."

Waylon couldn't believe Colton was sitting in his bar. At first, seeing him there had caused his heart to skip a beat. Then he'd noticed the handsome, steel-gray-haired man sitting across from him, and he'd wanted to throttle the guy.

It didn't make sense. The guy's hair wasn't even gray as in he was old and the color was gone. The stranger—Westram—was probably in his early thirties, and his hair was completely natural. Waylon felt damn certain of that.

Okay, it did make sense. Waylon wanted to be the man sitting across from Colton enjoying a meal. The problem was, he couldn't.

Because I'm dating someone else. Someone jealous and petty and who wants to track my every damn move.

Which made his own feelings of jealousy that much more difficult to deal with. Then, as if Colton could read his mind, he'd told Waylon that Westram was a friend, and it wasn't a date. Something in his gut had unfurled. Although, Waylon had still wished he was the one sitting across from Colton.

As Waylon carried the beers back to the two men, he tried to figure out what, if anything, he should do about all this.

Do I tell Colton to leave me alone? Do I ignore what's between us? Maybe I should . . . god, do I really want to chance jumping from one controlling boyfriend to another?

After all, it was obvious that Colton was stalking him.

Wasn't it? Or is it truly a coincidence that Colton showed up while I was working?

Waylon's head was spinning, and he didn't know what to do or think. If his buddies could see him now, they would laugh their asses off. He'd been friends with Jake, Petey, and Link for over two decades.

They'd all grown up together in their neighborhood. Even when Petey's mother had moved them after the divorce, they'd still stayed close enough to remain in the same school. His buddies called often, but he hadn't seen them in a couple of weeks.

Huh. That's telling.

When the man at the booth to the left slid out and stood, Waylon nearly slammed right into him. He deftly stepped aside and moved around him. The man's eyes widened, and he murmured an apology before heading toward the hallway leading to the men's room.

Waylon focused on the job as he placed the beers and waters before Colton and Westram. Then he added a basket of warm, complimentary tortilla chips with two types of salsa — one more spicy and the second mild but chunky. "Here you go, guys. Your appetizer should be up shortly." He tucked the platter under his arm as he glanced between them, unable to help how his gaze lingered over Colton's warm dark eyes. "Have you decided on a meal, or do you need more time?"

"I think we've decided," Colton replied, his husky purr sending need pulsing through Waylon's veins that was so damn tough to ignore. "Westram?"

"Yep." Westram tapped the menu. "I'll take your double bacon cheeseburger with everything, and upgrade me to the bottomless cheese fries."

Waylon quickly wrote down the order. At the same time, he swallowed quickly, forcing moisture into his dry throat. He didn't bother telling the guy that the only time he'd seen someone make it through one helping of the cheese fries let alone asked for a second helping had been from a four hundred-plus pound guy who took up the entire bench seat.

Licking his lips, Waylon smiled at Colton. "And you, Colton?"

Appearing pleased to be addressed by name, Colton pointed at the sizzling fajita entre. "I'd like to have this with all three meat options . . . beef, chicken, and shrimp. I'd also like extra guacamole and sour cream."

"Oh, good choice," Waylon replied with a nod. "I'll get those started for you."

"And another beer," Westram cut in, setting down his

nearly empty mug.

Waylon chuckled, impressed. "You got it."

As Waylon walked away, he heard Colton snort. "Thirsty, Wes?"

"Yep. Watching you drool over—" Then they were out of earshot.

Too bad.

After putting in the order, Waylon made the rounds of his tables. All the while, he struggled with not constantly glancing at Colton. He drew a fresh beer for one table, then picked up another patron's empty strawberry lemonade glass and went into the back to prepare another. When Waylon was finished with that, he noticed Colton's appetizer order was ready.

Using a tray, Waylon placed the lemonade, the appetizer, and Westram's freshly poured beer on it. He handed off the strawberry lemonade first. Then he headed to Colton's table, and if his stomach tipped and tilted a little when the Hispanic man smiled in greeting at him, he wasn't gonna tell.

"Have you had your break already?" Colton asked as he pulled one of the small plates toward himself. He grinned up at him. "Not sure what your shift here is, but I'd love to sit with you if you have a fifteen-minute break or something."

Waylon opened his mouth, his surprise getting the better of him, and he stated, "I have a twenty-minute break coming up in a little over half an hour." He glanced toward Westram. "But what about . . ." Not knowing how he should finish that—*the fact that I have a boyfriend* or *the fact that you're here with a buddy*—Waylon trailed off.

Westram grabbed a couple of the eggrolls as he claimed, "Oh, I'll move to the bar, man. Just set me up with a fresh beer and more chips and salsa and I'll vedge with the boob tube or a book."

Waylon peered back at Colton, lifting both brows in question.

Colton chuckled under his breath. "It's true. Westram may look like a broad-shouldered brute, but he's a total book-worm."

His mouth full of eggroll, Westram just nodded and winked.

"O-Okay. I'll join you." It might not be wise, but he wanted to.

"I look forward to it," Colton stated, then grabbed a couple of eggrolls for himself.

Waylon returned to work.

Ten minutes before his expected break time, Waylon put in an order for a bowl of queso. It was an appetizer cheese dish that also contained a bit of ground beef and chili. Eaten as a dip with tortilla chips, he thought Colton would enjoy trying it.

Shortly after that, his supervisor—Tiffany—told him to make a final sweep of his tables before going on break. "I'll watch your tables while you relax."

"Thanks." Waylon couldn't remember the last time he'd looked forward to such an impromptu meal.

Not a date.

Maybe if Waylon reminded himself of that enough, he would believe it. He dismissed his unease—*I'm on break at work, eating with a friend*—and quickly checked everything out. Then, as Westram had suggested, he poured the man a fresh beer and grabbed him a basket of fresh chips and salsas.

Waylon took those to Westram, who appeared completely comfortable and at ease moving his remaining cheese fries to the bar and sitting at the bar by himself. "Thanks, man. Have fun." As he pulled out his phone and began to read, he munched on the chips and salsa.

Even as he couldn't believe he was about to ask it, Waylon asked, "Should I put in another order for cheese fries? My substitute, Tiffany, will bring it out in around ten."

Westram grinned widely. "Yeah, thanks!"

Returning to the kitchen for not only a strawberry lemonade of his own but his dish of queso and chips, Waylon put in his order for a bottomless cheese fry refill. He had no clue where the slender, toned man was putting it all. The man must have had a hollow leg, as his mother would say.

After getting his own things together, Waylon took a fortifying breath, then returned to the dining area. He returned Colton's smile as he placed everything on the table where Westram had been. Then he tucked the tray behind the bar before seating himself across from Colton.

"Thank you for joining me," Colton murmured, smiling warmly at him. "How's your shift going?"

"Good, good," Waylon replied, sliding the dip to the middle of the table. "Quiet, but that's to be expected on a Wednesday afternoon. It'll probably pick up in another hour."

"Glad to hear it. I hope I'm not interrupting too badly."

Waylon shook his head, smiling upon seeing Colton's concerned expression. "No, this is pleasant." He pointed at the queso dip. "And you remember when I told you I'm mostly gluten-free? This is my guilty secret." Winking, Waylon picked up a tortilla chip and scooped it through the hot dip. "Queso cheese with spicy chili meat. It's amazing." As Waylon lifted his queso-covered chip to his mouth, he encouraged, "You need to try it."

To Waylon's pleasure, Colton obeyed. Waylon had already swallowed and scooped up some more when he watched the other man pop the chip and dip into his mouth. The hum of appreciation went straight to his balls.

Oh, holy shit.

"Gods, you're right. This is wonderful."

Feeling his blood heat and his arousal churning through his veins, Waylon knew he was in trouble. For a few minutes, he did his best to ignore it. Instead, he smiled, nodded, and focused on eating.

"Well, this looks cozy."

Waylon whipped his head around. He nearly choked on his queso-coated chip upon spotting Richard standing a few feet away. His boyfriend had his legs braced apart and his arms crossed over his chest.

Okay. Now I'm in deep shit.

Except, Waylon had no clue how to fix it . . . or even if he wanted to.

CHAPTER FIVE

Colton noticed Waylon's scent went from relaxed and content with just a hint of nerves, to panicked, guilty, and just plain fearful.

Turning his attention to the speaker, Colton recognized him — Richard, the boyfriend.

Damn.

Upon taking in Richard's combative stance and accusing expression, Colton realized the man was gearing up to make a scene. No way would that be good for Waylon while at his work. Colton spotted how Waylon's mouth opened, closed, then opened again, but no actual words came out.

Maybe I can help diffuse the situation.

Just because Colton wanted Waylon to dump Richard didn't mean he wanted to have their issues aired in a restaurant.

Colton smiled warmly at Richard even though it was the last thing he wanted to do. "Hi. Richard, isn't it?" He held out his hand. "I recognized Waylon from the park. You were there, too." Since Richard hadn't bothered to take his hand, just continued to glare at him, Colton snapped his fingers as if figuring something out. "You said you were his boyfriend." When the slender human's eyes narrowed, he shrugged. "I understand what this could look like, but it's not."

Richard's lip-gloss painted lips curved into a sneer. "You think I'm stupid?" he shrieked, anger filling his tone. His sparking gaze focused on Waylon. "How long have you been sneaking around with this man behind my back?" Richard

39

pointed at Colton. "How long have you been cheating on me?"

Before Waylon could say anything, in his defense or not, Richard continued. "Did he suck you off in the bathroom at *World of Aquatica*? Was that a hook-up?" Scoffing, the sound full of malice, he added, "I bet that's why you didn't want me afterward. You'd already gotten some."

Colton didn't know how it was possible, but somehow, the skin of Waylon's dark-brown cheeks managed to take on a slightly pinkish hue. The scent of embarrassment and humiliation flooded the room. His white-knuckled grip on his glass betrayed how tightly he was holding his strawberry lemonade, and Colton feared he would shatter the glass and hurt himself.

While Colton had never considered his seahorse an aggressive animal, right now, he had the strangest urge to whap Richard across the face with his tail. Not that it would do much good. His seahorse was tiny . . . only six inches from nose to tail-tip.

"I think you really need to calm down, dude," Westram stated, having sidled over.

"Who the fuck are you to tell me what to do?" Richard snorted as he looked Westram's strong, wiry frame up and down. "You think you're gonna beat the shit out of me because I'm gay? Bring it, and I'll sue your ass for every penny you got."

Westram rolled his eyes as he slid into the booth seat beside Colton, who instantly made room for him. "You make way too many assumptions, pal." He slung his arm over the back of the booth behind Colton as he grinned crookedly at Richard. "You know what they say about people who assume things. It makes an ass out of you and me."

"Did you just call me an ass?" Richard gasped, his cheeks turning red.

Westram rolled his eyes. "Yeah. Assume."

Richard waved his hand between them. "Don't think this little display is fooling me," he said, his voice rising as he returned his focus on Waylon. "I know you've been cheating."

Waylon finally found his voice after clearing his throat. "Thanks for the company during break," he murmured, sliding to the edge of the booth and rising. "But I better get back to work." He turned to Richard and met his gaze. "I never cheated on you, Richard. These are friends." He waved to indicate Colton and Westram. "We were just talking."

As much as Colton hated being relegated to *a friend*, he liked seeing Waylon stand up for himself.

"Liar!" Richard shrieked. "I catch you red-handed, and still you lie. You're a dumbass good for nothing but your big dick. You—"

"That's enough," bellowed a heavy-set tan-skinned man in dress slacks and a red shirt, except he wore a tie and sported an air of self-importance. "You will leave this establishment and take your crude language with you." He pointed toward the front door. When Richard opened his mouth as if to argue, the man threatened, "Or I'll call the cops and have you arrested."

Richard still looked mutinous, but he jerked a nod. Then he glared at Waylon and growled, "We'll talk about this later."

Waylon shook his head. "No, we won't. Don't call me, Richard." Moving away from everyone and toward the back, he added, "We're through. Leave me alone."

"What?" Richard lunged toward Waylon, but Westram was quicker.

Westram inserted himself between Waylon and Richard, holding up his hand, palm out in a warning to back off. "Waylon asked you to leave him alone."

With one more scathing stare to Westram, Waylon, and Colton, Richard pivoted on his expensive shoes and flounced out of the restaurant.

Huh. I didn't know men could flounce.

Colton didn't know if he was impressed or put off.

"I'll get back to work. Sorry, Mister Macinaw," Waylon stated in a subdued tone.

"No, Waylon. Clear out your locker and head out." Mister Macinaw crossed his arms over his chest and scowled up at Waylon. "Your disruptive influence has no place here, and this is the last straw."

"Y-You're firing me?" Waylon gaped, clearly shocked.

Colton rose and drew closer. "Wait a minute," he began softly. "None of this was Waylon's fault."

Hell, I'm more at fault than Waylon.

Not that he mentioned that.

"There's enough fault to go around," Mister Macinaw claimed, curling his lip as he glanced between Colton and Westram. He stared at them distastefully. "Tiffany is bringing your check and some boxes. Please leave the premises as swiftly as possible."

Westram growled low in his throat, and Mister Macinaw whipped around to face him. The human backed up a step, then straightened to his full height while adjusting his tie. "Do I need to call the cops on you all, too?"

"No," Colton quickly replied. "We're going."

Colton spotted Tiffany and thanked her for the check. After a quick scan of it, he handed her his credit card. Then he used the boxes she'd also given him and, with Westram's help, packed up their leftovers.

By the time the shifters made it outside, Colton saw that Waylon's truck was gone. After stowing the boxes on the back floorboard, he climbed behind the wheel. He sighed deeply, then peered Westram's way.

"That is not how I'd hoped this would turn out," Colton mused softly. "Thank you for trying to help diffuse the situation."

Westram nodded. "Sorry it didn't work." His stormy gray eyes narrowed. "So, uh, what did you want to happen here today?"

Colton shrugged. "To be honest, not entirely sure. Just see him. Have him see me. Talk." Sliding the key into the ignition, as he started his vehicle, he added, "Maybe set up another not-date."

"Not-date?" Westram chuckled. "What is that?"

"Two buddies who like each other but there's no possibility of a kiss at the end of their time together." Colton saw Westram's brows lift as a smirk curved his lips, and he shrugged. "It's time for us to hang out and get to know each other without the pressure of calling it a date or possibly giving in to our attraction."

"Personally, giving in to the attraction is half the fun," Westram commented, wrinkling his nose. Then he grinned. "You did get one thing out of this, though. Waylon dumped Richard."

For a couple of seconds, Colton felt his heart soar. His mate was now free to pursue. Then his excitement plummeted.

"Yeah, but my actions were part of him losing his job," Colton pointed out. "How the hell is he ever going to forgive me?"

"Blowjobs. Lots and lots of blowjobs," Westram said on a laugh. Colton began to roll his eyes, but the enforcer quickly added, "And a new job."

Whipping his focus to Westram, Colton cocked his head. "Huh?"

"He's your mate!" Westram patted Colton's arm. "Come on. Let's get back to Aquatica and tell Kaiser and William what happened. I bet they'll have a job lined up for him in no time."

Colton nodded as he maneuvered his vehicle out of the parking lot, hoping the enforcer was right.

Waylon paced his front room, rubbing the back of his neck and bald head. His heart hammered in his chest, and he repeatedly shook his head. The adrenaline coursing through his body made his muscles bunch, and he shook his arms and flexed his fingers in an effort to relieve the discomfort.

The way he felt reminded him of when his high school football team had won the state championship. He'd been exhausted but had still needed an outlet for the excitement thrumming through his body. That time, he'd found a hot little band geek to fuck.

Can't do that now.

Pausing, Waylon brought up the image of Colton—his lithe body, twinkling brown eyes, and mischievous smile. His cock thickened in his board shorts, and he couldn't resist cupping himself. With just the thought of the sexy man, his body became primed to take the guy.

So odd.

While Waylon had always had a pretty impressive sex drive, his reaction time to Colton was damn faster than anything he'd ever experienced. It didn't help that Monday and Tuesday evening, when he'd spent time with Richard, he hadn't been able to get it up. No wonder the man thought he had been cheating on him.

His ringing phone drew his attention.

Richard . . . again.

Waylon had ignored four phone calls from the man in the last half hour. He had no idea how Richard knew he wasn't still at work, since he'd been scheduled for another three hours. Figuring it meant that Richard was watching him, he felt a crawling sensation trickle up his spine.

Besides, there was no other way for Richard to have known he was spending his break with another man.

That returned his thoughts to Colton. The man was sex on

a stick and had made his interest known. Except, after seeing how he allowed Richard to walk all over him, Colton probably wouldn't want him anymore.

God, I need to do something to get out of my head.

His phone rang again.

Waylon rejected the incoming call, then made an outgoing one of his own.

"Hey, Way," Jake greeted jovially. "How's it hangin', man? Aren't you supposed to be at work?"

"I got fired," Waylon told him bluntly. "Wanna go surf?"

"Fuck yeah. I think Petey may be off right now, too, but Link's out of town. I'll give him a ring and meet you at Yellow Fork Beach. Say . . . twenty minutes?"

Waylon let out the breath he'd been holding. At least one thing in his life always remained the same. Jake worked from home as an erotic romance writer, and he always seemed available to drop everything and hang out. While Waylon didn't know how Jake met his deadlines, he wouldn't look a gift horse in the mouth.

"Thanks. See you soon."

"Yep." Jake's tone turned serious, which was rare. He was the happy-go-lucky one. "And you're gonna tell us what the hell happened."

Nodding, even though his buddy wouldn't see it, Waylon agreed. "You got it."

Jake grunted, then the line disconnected.

Waylon quickly gathered what he needed, then carted everything down his apartment stairs to his truck. He loaded up and started on his way. As he drove to the beach, he thought about the last time he'd gone surfing just a couple of days before . . . and his dick plumped in his shorts.

"Son of a bitch," Waylon grumbled, reaching down to adjust himself. His phone rang, and when he spotted the display and Richard's name there, his erection died a quick death. "Probably for the best."

Reaching the beach first, Waylon parked and unloaded. Then he found a dressing room and changed. By the time he returned to his truck to get his board, he'd spotted both Jake and Petey's vehicles.

Leaning on his truck, Waylon waited.

A couple of minutes later, Jake and Petey appeared, bumping shoulders and laughing about something. When they spotted Waylon, both men grinned and began jogging toward him. Jake's shoulder-length, dark-brown hair bobbed in the wind, while Petey's black hair, pulled back in a tiny ponytail, barely moved.

Jake reached him first. He slammed into Waylon, giving him a one-armed bro-hug. His buddy's six-foot-one, well-muscled body felt warm against Waylon's own.

Then it was Petey's turn. Before the six-foot, wiry man had even pulled away, he was saying, "What the hell happened? What are you up to?"

Waylon sighed deeply, which caused the other men to exchange worried glances. Then, as Waylon hefted his board and turned toward the beach, his buddies grabbed their own boards and fell into step on either side of him. Trusting his friends to be honest, Waylon shared everything.

While the trio waited for the next good wave, their stomachs on their boards, Jake and Petey took turns asking questions. It took a fair amount of time to get all the story out, since they were constantly being interrupted. Waylon didn't mind, seeing as every few minutes, he could shut his brain down and let his body take control.

Finally, the group trudged back to shore and plopped down in the sand to rest. "I'm real sorry to say this," Jake began slowly. "But moving on from Richard is probably a good thing."

Petey was nodding, then added, "He wasn't very good for

you. Controlling and jealous."

Jake bumped his shoulder into Waylon's. "Kept you from your friends. Alienating you."

Waylon let out a deep sigh as he nodded. "I'd started noticing that over the past month but put up with it for the sex," he admitted, wincing.

"Thinkin' with your dick, eh, Big W?" Petey laughed as he elbowed him. Then he asked, "What about this Colton guy? You're definitely attracted to him. And even if he doesn't want a relationship for the long haul, from the way you talk about your chemistry, bet he'd be a great rebound fuck."

To Waylon's surprise, he had to fight back a growl at hearing Petey talk about Colton that way.

Weird.

Clearing his throat, Waylon muttered, "Doubt he's interested after seeing how I let Richard walk all over me."

Jake scoffed. "Eh, then he ain't worth your time." Waggling his brows, he gave Waylon a playful lecherous once over. "But I bet that won't make a difference."

"Just remember, dude. You're not having any more relationships with assholes who try to keep you away from your friends," Petey declared, his tone serious. "We're your family. So if you end up really liking the guy, we get to meet him and decide."

Waylon nodded. "Agreed."

"Now that we've got that settled"—Jake jumped to his feet—"let's surf some more."

Although Waylon wasn't certain he had anything settled at all, he allowed his friends to drag him back into the ocean.

CHAPTER SIX

Colton tapped his forefingers on his thigh as he listened to Waylon's phone ring. Thinking he would have to leave a message, he thought swiftly about what he wanted to say . . . and how. When Waylon answered, Colton froze in surprise.

"Colton?"

Waylon quietly saying his name, a question in his tone, pulled Colton's head out of his ass.

"Hi, Waylon," Colton greeted in a subdued tone. "Thank you for taking my call. I wanted to apologize."

"Apologize." Waylon sounded confused. "Why would you need to do that?"

Colton sighed softly, rubbing his palm over his jaw. "If I hadn't stopped by the restaurant, you wouldn't have lost your job. I—"

Pausing, Colton tried to figure out how to share his need to see and care for Waylon without explaining shifters. He knew their relationship wasn't anywhere near that, yet. Besides, there was no way Waylon would believe without proof. His mate would think he was nuts.

Waylon scoffed softly, the sound almost kind. "That wasn't your fault. If it hadn't been this incident, then it would have been something else." The sound of Waylon's big body moving on fabric betrayed that he was settling on his recliner. "Manager Macinaw has been looking for a reason to fire me for months. Ever since he found out I was gay. The guy is a grade-A homophobic asshole."

Colton growled softly under his breath. "He can't fire you

for your sexual orientation."

"No, he couldn't, but he can fire me for causing a disturbance, for being late, or for making mistakes at the job," Waylon explained. "Richard has been needy lately. Taking up a lot of my time, and I've been tired and done all those other things. So . . . like I said. Just a matter of time."

Grimacing upon hearing Waylon mention his boyfriend, Colton couldn't help himself. "Did you mean it?"

"Mean what?"

"That you dumped Richard?"

"Yeah. At least something good came out of that."

Colton couldn't suppress his surprise . . . or his glee. He grinned. "Does that mean you're gonna accept my offer for a date?"

Waylon sighed. "Not right away, Colton."

Swallowing hard, Colton felt as if his heart constricted in his chest. He focused on the intonation. *Right away.* That meant there was a possibility for the future. To Colton's relief, Waylon continued to speak.

"Look. I know we have chemistry," Waylon rumbled in his deep voice. He sighed into the phone, sounding tired. "But I need a little time to get my head on"—he chuckled roughly for a second, then finished—"not straight, exactly, but you know what I mean."

"I do know, and I'll give you as much time as you need," Colton assured. He desperately wanted to reach through the phone line and hug his exhausted sounding mate. "Just remember one thing. My feelings on the matter aren't going to change, no matter how long that is."

"You can't know that," Waylon countered, sounding confused.

Colton chuckled as he rested the back of his head against his sofa's cushion. Staring at the ceiling, he countered, "I think we both understand how rare a chemistry like ours is, so . . .

we'll continue to be friends, and when you're ready for more, all you have to do is let me know." Unwilling to keep listening to Waylon's doubts, Colton hurried and said, "Apologizing and asking if you're really single now weren't the only reasons I called, though."

"Oh?" Waylon cleared his throat. "Then, why?"

"I wanted to make it up to you for losing your job, so I found you another one" — Colton hesitated, then added — "if you want it."

His disbelief clear, Waylon muttered, "It's only been five hours. What could you have possibly lined up so quickly?" After another second, he added, "You know I'm not a mechanic. I don't have that kind of training."

"I know, Waylon." Colton didn't care for the disparaging note in Waylon's tone. His mate should never think he wasn't smart just because he didn't have academic pursuits. Instead of sharing his opinion, Colton told him, "I don't know if you enjoyed your job at *Scooter's Bar and Grill*, other than your asshole boss, of course, but — "

"Don't tell me you can get me back on there," Waylon cut in. "Even if Mister Macinaw offered, I wouldn't go back."

"Not there," Colton told him, stopping that line of thought. "There's a bar and waiter opening at *World of Aquatica*'s restaurant *Mini Barrier Reef Cantina*. That's the restaurant we bumped into each other at."

Colton held his breath, praying Waylon would accept. The position would keep his human close enough for him to see on a regular basis. Plus, there would be plenty of other shifters and mates around if there was ever a problem.

"Really?" A hint of interest filled Waylon's voice. "I admit, I don't have a lot of ambition." He'd said the words quietly, as if he was worried about how Colton would take them. "I just want to make enough money to live within my means and have plenty of time to enjoy surfing and spending time with friends."

Even though Colton didn't point out that Waylon didn't say anything about finding love and companionship, he was thinking it.

Damn Richard.

It seemed the man had soured his mate on the idea of finding a partner.

That's okay. I can wait. Especially if I can keep him close.

"There's nothing wrong with that goal," Colton told him, rubbing his free hand over his aching heart. After only a few days, he cared so much for his mate already. "Can I tell Eban that you'll be around tomorrow for an interview? He's head of security and would escort you."

After a moment of silence, Waylon told him, "How about on Monday morning?"

Colton wanted to ask what Waylon intended to do for the next four days, but he resisted. His mate needed time. He would give it to him.

"Sounds good." It didn't. Not really, but Colton couldn't admit that, yet. "I'll text you the time as soon as they tell me."

"Thanks." Waylon cleared his throat, then added, "And thanks for the help. I'll talk to you later."

Before Colton could think of a way to extend the conversation, Waylon hung up.

Resting the phone on his thigh, Colton sighed deeply. His seahorse trilled in the back of his mind, the sound full of sadness.

He assured his animal that he would be back.

Colton had to believe that. In the meantime, he would focus on work. There were always cars to fix.

"He's in love with you."

Waylon whipped his head around and stared at Link. His friend grinned broadly, waggled his reddish-blond brows, then jumped, his feet landing on his surfboard. All Waylon could do was watch as Link surfed away . . . until the wave swamped him, and he went under.

Shit!

Righting his board, Waylon climbed back on. As he waited for another perfect wave to ride, he realized Link had said that at that exact moment on purpose. It gave him time to sit there and stew over the comment.

Link couldn't be right? Could he?

Over the past three weeks, Colton had surfed and hung out with Waylon and his buddies on numerous occasions. He seemed to fit in well, his friends exchanging just as many texts with Colton as they did with Waylon. They'd even spent weekends at car shows, fairs, and shacked up with their cars at Petey's.

His friend had inherited an old home north of town that had a huge workshop from his grandparents when they'd passed almost five years ago.

Colton had been impressed with the space, and he'd offered to do some tinkering on all their vehicles. When they'd offered to pay him for his time, he'd flipped them the bird and ordered, "Just pay for parts. I'm a mechanic. This is fun for me." Then Colton had gotten Jake's old *Dodge Challenger* running better than it ever had.

Spotting a wave to ride, Waylon judged the distance, then leaped. He balanced on the board and rode the wave toward shore. Just as the wave began to dissipate and he readied for a graceful leap off, Waylon spotted Colton swimming out with Jake.

The view of Colton's ass flexing as his legs pumped distracted Waylon, and his board slid out from under him. Waving his arms, he flopped into the water. He found his feet fast enough, and he bobbed up just in time to see Link and Petey laughing at him.

Waylon growled as he stalked up the shallows toward his

two friends. As soon as he reached them, he punched Link on the upper arm. Link howled, his laughter intensifying.

"You are such an asshole," Waylon grumbled before fixing a scowl on Petey. "You know what he said to me?"

Petey smirked. "Yep, and I agree with him." He rolled one slender shoulder. "Jake agrees, too. Stop playing hard to get, and fuck his hard ass." Waggling his brows, Petey added, "You know you want to."

Waylon groaned. His blood heated just at the thought of boning Colton. The more time he spent with him, the more his fingers twitched with need and his mouth watered with his desire to taste.

Unfortunately, while Waylon spotted Colton giving him the occasional appreciative glance, he never so much as touched him.

"I don't know about that," Waylon murmured, watching the handsome Hispanic man jump onto his board and glide along the way as if one with the ocean. "He doesn't do much more than offer an occasional glance."

"Didn't you say that was what he told you he'd do?" Link nudged his shoulder. "Give you time to recover from Dickwad's assholishness?"

Waylon knew his buddy referred to Richard. They'd taken to calling him that the day he'd told them that he'd dumped the bastard. Realizing he'd forgotten he'd shared that with his friends, he nodded.

He's left me alone just like he promised.

Damn.

"Here they come," Petey stated, tipping his chin in the direction of Jake and Colton. "Go get your man, Way."

Just hearing his friend's encouragement that he get his man, Waylon's blood flowed south. The idea had a predictable reaction on his body. His dick thickened, which was damn uncomfortable in his wetsuit.

Link laughed, knocking his shoulder. "You look like you

could use ten minutes." He looked down pointedly as he patted Waylon on the shoulder. "We'll grab Jake, and you can hit the head for something other than its intended use."

Petey joined in the laughter as he added, "Have fun!"

Even as Waylon shook his head at the pair of yahoos, he joined them in heading toward Jake and Colton. Upon seeing Colton's confused expression as they tromped through the surf, he hoped his friends were correct. Otherwise, Waylon would be damn embarrassed.

Link beckoned to Jake. "Come on, man. Waylon needs a sec with Colton." After a wink, he added, "They'll meet us for pizza at *Luigi's* shortly."

Jake glanced between them, then offered a wide grin. "Sure thing. See ya in a bit, guys."

Colton leveled a questioning look Waylon's way. Opening his mouth and lifting a brow, he started, "What—"

Waylon didn't let him finish. Grabbing the back of Colton's head, he yanked him forward. He slammed his mouth over the other man's. Taking advantage of the fact that the smaller man's mouth was open, Waylon thrust his tongue inside, finally giving in to his need to taste the man.

The flavor of saltwater mixed with something decidedly masculine burst across Waylon's tongue. Delving deep, he growled, searching for more. As he teased along Colton's appendage, for one horrifying second, he realized the other man wasn't kissing back.

In the next instant, that changed.

Colton fed Waylon a groan as he gripped his hip with his free hand and pushed his mouth into Waylon's own. Their boards bumped against their sides as Waylon used his hold on the other man's neck to tilt his head and push deeper. His senses swam as his cock throbbed with need at just the tongue-tangle.

The sound of wolf whistles rent the air. Then someone hollered, "Get a room," sounding amused. Unfortunately, for every understanding person, there was another who didn't . . . and that person shouted, "Faggots!"

"Fuck off, asshole." That was Jake's voice, and he sounded angry.

Damn it.

Waylon eased the kiss to an end. After sparing a smile for a surprised and aroused looking Colton, he glanced around. Spotting Jake advancing on a red-faced man whose sneering visage glanced between them and Jake, Waylon hollered, "Leave it, Jake. That asshole ain't worth it."

"Yeah, walk away, cocksuckers," the moron yelled, crossing his arms over his broad torso. "You all couldn't take me and my buddies, anyway."

A trio of thug-like brutes strode over to stand behind the loud-mouth.

"Knock it off. All of you!" a life-guard called from the tower. "If you can't be civil, beat it."

Waylon waved. "We were leaving anyway, Ned."

Ned brightened. "Oh, hey, Waylon. Didn't realize it was you. Congrats on the hot new boyfriend." Snorting, he continued, "You were never meant for a stuck-up snob who couldn't handle a little sand on his feet."

"Figures you're a fag, too," the mouthy man stated, curling his lip. "Come on. Let's leave this beach full of homos."

At least the fight had been averted.

Turning toward Colton, Waylon led the way toward the changing rooms. "Come on," he urged, holding his soon to be lover's hand. "It's time we talk."

"Not sure I'm in the mood to talk," Colton murmured huskily, clearly being honest. "But if you say so."

Waylon laughed as he headed into a room and pulled Colton in behind him. After locking the door, he wrapped his arms around the man. "Thank you for your patience, Colton."

Waylon spread his legs and leaned against the wall, lowering his stance. "Do you still want me? Because I want you."

He figured he should just lay it out there.

Holding his breath, Waylon waited for a response.

CHAPTER SEVEN

Colton let out a low groan. Knowing they were in the middle of a public place—even if they were behind a locked door—he knew being quiet was necessary. Still, with the scent of Waylon's arousal flooding the small room, his mouth watered and his dick throbbed.

A glance down showed Colton that Waylon was in the same predicament. "Yeah," he whispered. "I want you." Gripping the zipper of his wetsuit, he quickly yanked it down. Shoving it off until it rested just below his balls, Colton gripped his bobbing shaft. "This is what you do to me every fucking time you look at me, every time I think about you, any time you're near."

Resting his hand on Waylon's ripped stomach, Colton carefully avoided the huge swell pressing against the front. "Can I see what I do to you?"

Waylon bit his lower lip, probably to keep in a moan of his own. Even as he nodded, he unzipped his own wetsuit. Pushing it down, he revealed his massive rod, swollen, dark, and leaking pre-cum.

"Oh, yeah," Colton muttered on a growl. Stepping between Waylon's thick thighs, he leaned against him. "Legs a little wider, if you can."

After Waylon had awkwardly obeyed, Colton levered against him. He had to stand on his toes due to the slight height difference, but when his mate palmed his ass with one meaty mitt, it made it easy. His erection, shorter and slenderer than Waylon's, pressed against his human's.

Waylon clamped his jaw together and arched against him. His hips bucking, he rocked his thick shaft against Colton's.

As much as Colton would love to have their first time slow and easy so he could worship Waylon's body, he knew that wasn't possible. They'd waited too long. His need to begin the bonding process rode him hard.

"Kiss me," Colton demanded, resting his hands on Waylon's bulging shoulders. "Please."

"Hell yeah," Waylon muttered, dipping his head.

Waylon sealed his lips over Colton's. Feeling his human shove his thick tongue into his mouth, he went with it. He teased, lapped, and sucked on the appendage.

Colton began rocking his hips. The glide of their shafts against each other soon became easy with the copious amounts of pre-cum they were both expelling. He moaned softly into Waylon's mouth, relishing the exquisite sensations rolling through his body in bliss-inducing waves.

Feeling the base of his spine tingle and his balls roll deliciously, Colton knew his orgasm approached. He didn't fight it. Instead, he rutted harder against his mate's exquisite body.

Breathing noisily through his nose, Colton fed Waylon a series of low grunts and groans as his release washed through him. He broke the kiss and gasped as he peered up at Waylon's heavy-lidded expression. His lips were kiss-swollen, and his features twisted into a feral curl.

Knowing that look from nearly two centuries of sex, Colton sank to his knees. He heard Waylon whimper, the sound incongruous coming from such a big man . . . and it was music to Colton's ears. Opening his mouth, Colton wrapped his lips around Waylon's mammoth shaft and swallowed it to the root.

Colton silently thanked his non-existent gag reflex, because his mate's dick was huge. As he bobbed on the thick length, he guessed it was at least an eleven-incher. Waylon's thighs trembled under his hands, and when Colton cupped his balls, he threw his head back and opened his mouth in a silent scream.

Pulse after pulse of thick cream flooded Colton's mouth. He nearly choked due to the volume of fluid, but he swallowed quickly and got it down. Pulling back just a little, he enjoyed the lightly salty, masculine flavor with just a hint of iron tang as the next couple of bursts landed on his tongue.

Gods, my mate was in need.

Colton continued to suckle gently as Waylon came down from his release. His abdominals twitched under his fingertips as he explored, and his thighs trembled. When Waylon finally began to soften, Colton allowed the tasty flesh to slip from between his lips.

Spotting a smear of red on Waylon's dick, Colton quickly licked it clean. He groaned under his breath when he realized it was his mate's blood. Somehow, they'd gotten too vigorous, and he'd drawn blood.

Oh, damn.

As Colton peered up Waylon's body, he watched his lover's closed eyelids flutter. It took a few seconds, but finally, he peered down at him. His lips were kiss-swollen, and his smile a little loopy-looking.

Okay . . . he's okay. Ha. More than okay.

"That's a damn fine look on you," Colton whispered, easing back to his feet. Rubbing his palms up and down Waylon's torso, tracing first his abdominals, then his pectorals, he murmured, "I sure hope you're going to allow me to put that expression on you again soon . . . and often."

Colton couldn't help how husky his voice had dropped. He'd waited so damn long, and finally, Waylon had given him permission to touch. He knew if they didn't get out of there soon, both their cocks would be hard again.

Waylon rested his hands on Colton's, squeezing his wrists

lightly. "Most definitely." Then his eyes narrowed as he rumbled, "As long as I get to return the favor."

"Mmm." Colton sucked in a harsh breath as he felt his blood heat anew. "Yes, please."

A soft tap sounded on the door, then Jake's voice called quietly, "Waylon. Ya gotta vacate, man. While we couldn't hear anything, this booth is still getting funny looks."

Colton grimaced. *Right.* Sex on a beach, even when guarded by Waylon's friends, wasn't a good thing.

"Sorry, Jake," Colton called back.

At the same time, Waylon chuckled and said, "Be right out."

"Unlock the door," Petey ordered. "We have your clothes."

They separated, then carefully cracked the door. Their clothes were tossed inside onto the wooden floor. After shucking their wetsuits, only bumping elbows and hips a minimum of times, they began tugging on clothes.

Seeing his seed all over Waylon's torso, a primal satisfaction filled Colton. Still, he cleared his throat and pressed his towel to his human's grooved abdomen. "Not sorry," Colton told Waylon with an eyebrow waggle as he cleaned him up. Then he did the same to himself.

Waylon's grin appeared smug as he reached out and swiped a couple of fingertips through the cum on Colton's chest. "Not sorry, either." Then he popped his fingers into his mouth and sucked them clean.

Colton froze, realizing what Waylon had just done.

Oh fuck. He just finished our bond.

Because Colton had accidentally bitten him and taken in his blood, and now that Waylon had accepted his seed, they were one.

Perhaps due to seeing his shocked expression, Waylon froze. "Guess I should have asked," he commented softly. "Are you not clean?"

Realizing what Waylon thought, Colton unstuck his

tongue from the roof of his mouth. "I'm clean. Just . . ." He forced a soft chuckle. "Didn't think you'd be into that, too."

"Because of my size?" Waylon asked.

While Waylon's voice sounded casual, his scent gave away his unease.

Shit. I didn't mean to unintentionally insult my mate. Damn. I have a lot to explain to him.

"I didn't mean to insult you, my mate," Colton murmured as he cradled Waylon's cheek. He mentally cringed at his slip of the tongue. "When it comes to sexual needs" — he waggled his brows, hoping to ease his lover's upset — "desires, we still have a lot to discuss."

To Colton's relief, it worked.

Waylon offered a small nod before pecking a kiss to his lips. "Sorry. A little sensitive about that." He threaded his fingers through Colton's hair. "My size has always made people jump to conclusions."

"Know you can ask me or tell me anything," Colton assured. "We'll work it out."

After Waylon nodded, Colton pecked another kiss to his lips, then eased away.

After they'd finished cleaning up and dressing, they slipped from the booth, their towels and wetsuits bundled in their arms. They received a number of knowing looks, sideways glances, and snickers from Waylon's buddies.

Colton just laughed along to the ribbing. He found he liked the guys. While he was still a little worried about how Waylon would deal with the secrecy paranormals needed, Colton hoped his mate eventually understood.

The group headed to *Luigi's Pizza and Pasta* restaurant. While waiting for a table, Waylon's buddies teased and joshed Waylon and Colton about finally getting together. Petey seemed exceptionally happy because the other pair handed over fifty bucks.

Evidently, they'd had a bet going about how long it would

take, and Petey had won.

After they'd ordered, Colton excused himself. "I need to go piss and wash my hands." Hearing the other men snicker, he just rolled his eyes and headed to the back.

Colton made use of the facilities, then crossed to the sink. After washing and drying his hands, he turned toward the door. He bit back a sigh upon seeing who stood just inside the door.

Really?

"Hello, Richard," Colton greeted levelly.

"You're going to walk away from Waylon," Richard ordered, crossing his arms over his chest.

Arching one brow, Colton leaned against the sink behind him as he dried his hands on a couple of paper towels. "Why would I do that?"

"As soon as you're out of the picture, Waylon will come back to me," Richard declared, thrusting a finger toward his chest. "You ruined everything! He's mine!"

"Waylon can make up his own mind about that," Colton countered. Having finished drying his hands, he waved the one not holding the paper towels and stated, "Out of the way, Richard. I'm ready for some pizza."

Richard curled his lip on a sneer. "So you need a little persuasion. That's okay." His blue eyes narrowed as an evil smile curved his lips. "I'd hoped that would be the case." Then he tapped twice on the door behind him.

Two hulking brutes entered the bathroom.

Colton sighed, more annoyed than scared. Both men were human, but explaining how he could beat the shit out of them would be tough.

Shoving his hands into his pockets, Colton fingered the phone in his right one. He called Eban on speed dial. Praying the great white shark shifter picked up swiftly, Colton tried to buy time. "Are these guys supposed to intimidate me, Richard?"

"No intimidation," Richard replied coldly. "They're just gonna beat the shit out of you."

"In *Luigi's Pizza and Pasta* bathroom?" Colton asked, giving his location. "You and your buddies plan to beat the shit out of me and leave me for dead?"

Richard laughed, sounding like a bad movie villain. "Yep. Then I'll get Waylon back, and I'm gonna turn him into my own personal fuck toy." He growled softly before saying, "For such a huge man, he takes it up the ass so beautifully."

Hearing Richard talk about fucking his mate made Colton see red. It didn't matter that he scented Richard's lie, or that Colton easily pegged Richard as a total bottom boy. It didn't even matter that it was obvious Richard said those things just to piss Colton off.

It worked.

"Well, at least now I know why you're a possessive asshole."

In hindsight, that probably hadn't been the best thing to say to buy more time.

Screaming for his grunts to get him, Richard pointed at him. The six-foot-four and five brutes lumbered toward him, and Colton prepared to kick ass.

Glancing at his diver's watch, Waylon wondered what was keeping Colton. The pizzas had just been delivered, and he didn't want them to get cold. After eating a couple of bites of his slice of three meat, double cheese, he set it down.

"I think I'm gonna go see what's keeping Colton," Waylon told his buddies as he wiped his fingers on a napkin. "Be right back."

Jake snickered as he quietly quipped, "Need to go hold his . . . hand?"

Waylon scowled and shook his head, but not for the reason

his buddies thought. "No, it's—" He rubbed the back of his neck as he stood. "Something's not right."

"Maybe he ended up with a cramp?" Petey rose from his seat. As a paramedic, he could help with that.

Unwilling to spend time speculating, Waylon headed toward the back of the restaurant. He reached the door and pushed . . . but it didn't budge. Having been to *Luigi's* more times than he could count, he knew it wasn't a single-person restroom. The only reason it should be closed was if it was being cleaned, and there was no sign outside the door to indicate that.

Knocking, Waylon called Colton's name. He heard a grunt, then his lover's voice call, "Just a sec, babe."

That was followed up by another voice that sent chills running down Waylon's spine.

Richard shrieked, "Don't call him that. He's mine! I told you to get him."

Then a series of thuds sounded through the door. A second later, the wall to Waylon's right shuddered.

"God, it sounds like a brawl in there. I'll get the guys. You break down the door." Petey's order jerked Waylon out of his shock.

"Right."

As his buddy scurried to the main room, Waylon back up a few steps as, from his many times of being inside, he mentally recalled where the locking latch was on the interior. He lowered his center of gravity, lined up his shoulder with the right side of the door—opposite where he knew the hinges were—and surged forward. The door latch popped, and he found himself skidding inside the room.

Waylon bounced against the sink on the other side of the room. Turning, he spotted Colton just as his lover managed to throw a guy twice his size across the space and into one of the two stalls. The second bruiser landed a punch to

Colton's face that should have cracked his jaw . . . except he did nothing more than rock back a step.

Then Colton came back swinging, easily setting the second man back on his heels.

Movement in his peripheral told Waylon that he wasn't the only one in shock upon seeing Colton's fighting prowess. His buddies were all clustered in the doorway. Plus, Richard peeked out of the second stall, his face red with fury.

Then Waylon spotted something else.

A low growl erupted from Waylon's throat as he rushed forward. The bang of the gun going off in an enclosed space echoed in his eardrums, making them ring. Pain stabbed through Waylon's side, drawing a sharp hiss from between his lips. That didn't stop him from grabbing Richard's out-stretched arm and slamming his wrist against the side of the bathroom stall with enough force to make him drop the weapon.

Waylon watched the handgun skitter under the stall wall toward the sinks, out of Richard's reach. Shoving his ex toward the wall, he pinned him there. When one of the smaller man's knees managed to clip where he'd been hit, Waylon gasped and fell backward.

Black spots danced across his vision, and he fell to his knees.

"Easy. Easy," Colton crooned, urging him to lean on him where he suddenly knelt beside him.

Huh. When did he get there?

"Okay, buddy. I gotta tear your shirt open, so I can take a look. Ready for that?"

As Waylon sagged against Colton, his eyes heavy-lidded, he mumbled. "Do it, Petey." Then he tucked his face into the crook of Colton's neck and inhaled deeply. Humming, he mumbled, "Damn, you smell good. Ocean spray and man. Love it."

"Is he gonna be okay?" That was Jake's voice, but Waylon

didn't have the energy to reassure him.

"There's an ambulance on the way," Link claimed. "He'll be fine. Right, Petey?"

"There's no exit wound," Petey muttered. "So an ambulance is good. We need to get him to the hospital as swiftly as possible and get the bullet out."

"He can't go to a standard hospital," a deep voice Waylon didn't recognize stated. "You all need to come with us."

"Now wait a minute," Petey began. "Who the hell are—"

"Please, Petey," Colton urged. "This is important. This is my boss, Alpha Kaiser, and that's Doctor Keller. Let him help. There are things you don't understand."

That was the last thing Waylon remembered before someone tried to move him, causing pain to stab through his torso, and he blacked out.

CHAPTER EIGHT

Colton sat on the bed in his bedroom at Aquatica, his back to the headboard, and he gently rubbed the smooth skin of Waylon's scalp. After so long pursuing his mate, there was something supremely satisfying about having his human there with him, even if he didn't care for how it had happened. His mate remained unconscious, but Doctor Keller had assured him that it was normal. The hammerhead shark shifter told him his mate would awaken in due time.

"Mmmm, that feels good."

Focusing on Waylon's face, Colton continued with his petting. "Good. You need a little feel good right now." After a second of hesitation, he asked, "Do you remember what happened?"

Waylon's face scrunched up for a few seconds before he huffed a sigh. "Fucking Richard shot me."

"Yeah."

"You were being attacked." Waylon's voice sounded thick and sleepy, but then he snapped open his eyelids. He glanced around frantically before focusing on him. "You were being attacked by two huge guys. Are you okay?" Then he frowned. "How did you throw that guy across the room?"

Even though Colton had hoped for a few more minutes before having to explain, he wasn't going to lie to Waylon. His mate needed to understand everything anyway. Besides, everything had already been explained to his three friends, and they'd accepted paranormals readily enough.

Evidently, Petey had seen a few things over the years as a

paramedic, so he'd been able to assure Jake and Link that stranger things were out there.

"Gods, why does every strange explanation begin with . . . now you may not believe me, but I swear it's the truth." Colton snickered at his stray thought, then shook his head as he spotted Waylon's confused expression. "Sorry. Just—" He sighed. Petting some more, Colton told him, "In a nutshell, Richard set those two goons on me. Except, he and his friends are human, and I am not, so he didn't count on the fact that I have increased strength and speed. Plus, I lived on the streets for decades, and even though I'm small, I know my way around a fight."

"Wait."

Waylon began to shift on the bed a bit, so Colton rested his free hand on his shoulder and pressed down. "Feel my extra strength, not allowing you to move?" When his mate's eyes widened and a flash of uncertainty filled the gray depths, Colton murmured, "I only stop you because if you move, you could tear the stitches. Doctor Keller and Petey had to dig the bullet out of your side."

To Colton's relief, Waylon relaxed. "Okay." His voice was a whisper, but he sounded steady enough. "You said Richard and his friends were human, and you have increased strength, which implies that you're not human."

Colton nodded, waiting for the actual question.

"Does that mean you're an alien?"

While Colton's initial reaction was to laugh, he squelched that response. That wouldn't help anyone. Instead, he shook his head.

"No, not an alien. Not in the sense you mean where I come from another planet." Colton hummed softly as he tipped his head back and forth a couple of times. "Until I met you, I never really thought about how to explain paranormals to a human before."

"Paranormal?" Then Waylon's eyes widened. "Jake writes about paranormals. Werewolves and vampires and stuff. Do you mean that kind of paranormal?"

Colton had been surprised when they'd talked to Waylon's friends and Alpha Kaiser and the others in the inner circle had realized Jake's creations weren't too far off the mark. He decided to use that to build on. "Your friend isn't too far off, although there are a few differences," Colton admitted. "Have you read much of his work?"

Waylon cleared his throat, but he nodded gamely. "Yeah. I've read his shit."

Grinning broadly, Colton winked. "Not shit. Westram loves him. When he realized who he was, he went a little fanboy."

Gaping up at him, Waylon muttered, "Seriously?"

Laughing softly, Colton nodded. "Oh yeah. Anyway, while paranormals don't live forever, and humans can't be turned into werewolves or vampires, a paranormal does bond for life with a fated soul mate." Narrowing his eyes, Colton rubbed Waylon's pectoral gently. "You are my fated mate, Waylon. I knew you the moment I scented you in that restaurant all those weeks ago. I have waited patiently, and now that we are together, I will devote my life to making you happy and keeping you safe and fulfilling your every need." Then Colton couldn't suppress his growl. "And we're bonded, so you'd better not be throwing yourself in front of any more gunmen."

For a long moment, Waylon remained silent. Colton knew he'd dropped a bomb on him. He did his best to wait patiently, hoping his mate wouldn't try to run or insist that he leave him alone.

"I-I have a couple of questions," Waylon started slowly, his gaze darting around the room.

That wasn't a good sign.

Gently scratching at Waylon's scalp once more—*oops,*

hadn't meant to stop — Colton stated, "I will tell you anything, my mate."

"Um . . . if you don't live forever, how long do you live?"

While not what he was expecting, Colton answered. "A shifter can live upward of five hundred years." Taking it a step further, he added, "That means your life will extend to match mine. I'm almost two hundred years old, so" — he scraped lightly over Waylon's scalp as he spoke — "if no crazy accidents happen, we'll live together for another three hundred years." Then Colton winced, needing to get it all out there. "Because we're bonded, if I die, there is a very high likelihood that you will, too." Nibbling his bottom lip, he mumbled, "Sorry. I meant to explain all that before we bonded, but —" He paused and heaved a sigh. "My bad. I didn't mean to nip your dick and drink your blood. Then you licked my cum off my chest and —" Colton could do little more than shrug.

Waylon barked a laugh, his eyes going wide. Then he snorted as he asked, "So Jake was right about bonding. Sex and blood?"

"Yes." Colton knew Jake had that part right.

"So . . . what's a shifter? Is it like a werewolf?"

"Not quite." For the next few minutes, Colton explained how shifting and sharing his spirit with an animal worked. Then he held his breath and waited with bated breath for Waylon's response.

Waylon opened his mouth . . . then closed it again. He really had no clue what to say. His buddy was right. Werewolves — or shifters — were real. Vampires were real, and so were soul mates or fated mates or whatever.

How fucked up is that?

Then Waylon tipped his head back and peered at Colton. He took in the worried crease of his lover's brows, and how he nibbled his bottom lip. All the while, he continued to massage, scratch, and rub Waylon's head, as if he could calm him through touch.

Maybe it all isn't so fucked up after all.

Because I want this man's touch and have since the moment I met him.

As odd as accepting that paranormals existed was, Waylon knew everything he'd been feeling finally made sense.

"So . . . um, can I ask what kind of shifter you are?" Waylon hazarded. "Or is that not polite?"

"Well, while you can't be asking that kind of question at random" — he winked — "you never know if an unknowledgeable human may overhear, but I'm happy to tell you. I share my spirit with a seahorse."

"Oh, wow! A seahorse. Really?" Waylon couldn't help it. He had to confirm.

Colton nodded. "And I'll be happy to show you someday, but now isn't the time. I'd need to be in saltwater."

Waylon immediately nodded vigorously. "Yeah. Totally." Then the pull in his side registered, as did his surroundings. "So, you didn't take me to the hospital. What happened after I passed out?"

For a second, Colton stared at him with narrowed eyes, as if trying to figure him out. Then he slowly told him how he'd called in the cavalry using his phone on speaker in his pocket, and others from his pod — since they were aquatic shifters — *weird* — came to help. Everyone had been taken back to *World of Aquatica* for processing.

Processing . . . so weird.

In Waylon's friends' cases, they'd been told everything and were now entrusted with the secret of paranormals. Waylon felt warmth fill him when Colton had explained that it had been at his urging, since over the weeks, he'd come to realize that those three men were Waylon's family. Plus, having friends to lean on in times of change was always a good thing, and Colton had wanted to give him that.

Waylon loved that Colton understood and hadn't tried to alienate him from his buddies as Richard did.

Speaking of which.

"And Richard and his brutes?" Waylon couldn't help but ask.

"Beta Williams is mated with the captain of a local police precinct, so he helped us smooth the way with charging them with assault and attempted murder." Colton winked. "I'm pretty certain they'll be going away for a long, *long* time."

Waylon's brows shot up. "You guys have ins... oh." Something clicked. "Wait a sec. Pod. As in whale pod."

Yeah, I like to watch documentaries.

"Beta, shifter, pod." Waylon narrowed his eyes. "So as a shifter, you have a local leader, or alpha who runs the show. The beta, or second-in-command, is mated to a police chief." Tipping his head to the side, Waylon couldn't help but ask, "If the beta is mated with a police chief, who's the alpha mated with? A governor?"

Colton shook his head. "No, it doesn't work like that. Fate picks mates based on personality and who would best complement us, making us a better person." Then his brows furrowed as he muttered, "Well, that's my opinion, anyway. Not like anyone has ever had the chance to talk to Fate and ask."

"So, why didn't I end up in the hospital? Just because of my friends?"

Shaking his head, Colton eased off the bed. "No." He whipped off his shirt and shorts. Then, before Waylon had a chance to enjoy checking out Colton's hard erection, he climbed under the blanket next to him. "You were brought here because, since you're mated with me, your healing has sped up."

Suddenly realizing that he wasn't in a whole lot of pain—little more than when he'd had his wrist in a brace when he'd sprained it his sophomore year of football—Waylon decided to take advantage. "Okay. Undress me."

Colton's eyes narrowed as a wide grin spread across his features. "So glad you decided to be on the same page." Then he eased the blanket to Waylon's waist, pausing to push down his board shorts.

Waylon spotted the bandage on the left side of his torso. He traced his forefingers along the top edge of it and asked, "So . . . how fast is my healing now?"

"Well, the bullet bounced off a rib, nicking and deflecting off it, but not cracking it. Once Doc Keller removed the bullet, chip, then stitched you up, it shouldn't be too long. Instead of a couple of weeks, maybe three to five days." Colton sighed deeply, shaking his head as he traced over the edge of Waylon's bandage. "I'm so damn sorry you were hurt. My heart felt nearly gutted when I saw the blood oozing from you."

Humming, Waylon decided nothing mattered but the man in bed with him. Ever since he'd met Colton, his life had slowly been improving. His sexy attentive lover had been ever-so-subtly trying to care for him since that day.

Well, and seducing me.

Waylon took in the concerned furrow of Colton's brows and how he leaned over him. Wanting more of his care, more of him, he knew he had to explain one more thing.

"In that changing shack, you mentioned still needing to share our sexual wants and desires," Waylon began slowly. Upon seeing Colton narrow his eyes as he nodded, he hurried to add, "I know it's bad form to mention past lovers, but Richard was a complete bottom boy, and I . . . I need more than that."

Colton's eyes widened for a second, then his lips curved into a wide smile. A smoldering heat entered his brown eyes, darkening them nearly to black. "You're a switch," he all but purred, rubbing his palm up Waylon's chest to flick a nipple.

Sparks flashed across Waylon's chest, and his breath caught in his throat. "Yes," he managed to whisper. "C-Can you give me what I need?"

Holding Waylon's gaze with his own hungry one, Colton nodded once, slowly. "My mate, I, too, am a switch." He rumbled his words as he leaned closer, half levering over him. "We will have all the time in the world to explore each other's bodies, but I can smell your need." Colton's gaze slid to where Waylon's cock tented his shorts. "And I wish to pleasure you." After once again locking his gaze with Waylon's, Colton huskily asked, "May I?"

Waylon groaned, his hips shifting restlessly on the mattress. It had been so damn long since he'd enjoyed the stretch and burn of penetration by another. His hole clenched in anticipation as Colton pushed his shorts down and off.

Once they were shoved off the side of the bed, Colton opened the nightstand drawer and grabbed a tube of lube. As he knelt beside Waylon, he rubbed over the unbandaged side of his abdominals as he asked, "Are you certain you're up for this?"

Laughing huskily, Waylon reached down and gripped his jutting shaft. He winked. "Oh, I'm definitely *up* for this," he told his lover playfully, not wanting him to worry.

Colton grimaced. "I really shouldn't. You were just shot."

For an instant, Waylon thought he would refuse. "Please." Anticipation already furled in his gut. "Please take me, Colton. Show me what I've been missing."

After licking his lips and swallowing hard enough to cause his Adam's apple to bob, Colton nodded once. "Okay."

Waylon happily spread his legs and watched with eagerness as Colton popped the cap on the lube and poured some on his fingers, then his bobbing slender erection. The first feel of Colton's fingers sliding into his long-neglected chute tore a hungry moan from his throat. Ignoring the twinge to his side, he rocked into each of Colton's finger-fucks.

My toys have nothing on the feel of Colton.

A few seconds later, when Colton levered over him and

bumped his cock head against Waylon's stretched hole, he paused long enough to whisper, "A shifter. No condom."

It took a second for Waylon's bliss-muddled mind to understand what Colton was tersely saying, but his man was patient. Waylon nodded. "No condom." Lifting his arms, he wrapped them around his much smaller lover's shoulders. "Please fill me. I need so badly."

Colton did as he asked, slowly easing inside his body.

Waylon groaned his pleasure, reveling in the feel of his shifter's erection sinking deep inside him. Not only that, but as Colton began to rut into him, filling him over and over, he knew, symbolically, he was accepting Colton and his new way of life.

As Colton began pegging Waylon's prostate again and again, sending his senses soaring, he knew nothing in his life had ever felt more right than being in the arms of the shifter who'd surfed into his life.

YOU MAY ALSO ENJOY THE FOLLOWING FROM EXTASY BOOKS INC:

Trill to Me Sweetly
Charlie Richards

Excerpt

Someone was following him. Someone he didn't recognize. In fact, two someones. Two someones who looked like muggers, with their dark hoodies and chains jangling from their jeans. Maybe it was stereotyping, but Bobby still debated his options — cut into an alleyway or start running. Both sucked.

When he felt the hand drop on his shoulder, Bobby squealed and did both. He yanked away from whoever the hell had touched him and started sprinting down the alley on his left. Bobby just knew if he could make it to the end, he could turn left, then right, and make it to a main road with taxis.

Sadly, at five foot seven he was short, which meant his legs were short, and the thugs caught up with him. A hand grabbed his sweatshirt, yanking him nearly off his feet. He gasped, losing his breath, but managed to regain his balance. That is, until whoever held him shoved him sideways into the wall.

He almost dropped his laptop case and scrambled to hang

onto it. Bobby had to wrap both arms around it to hold the old, heavy thing, causing him to scrape his knuckles on the building's stone walls.

"Now, why'd you have to go and run, dude?" one of his pursuers asked. "That only makes my buddy excited."

The other guy chortled, and it took everything in Bobby to turn around and face them. "Please, leave me alone," he whispered, his gaze darting back and forth between the two men. He clutched his laptop case to his chest like a shield.

"Aww, we ain't gonna hurt ya," said the first man again, obviously the duo's speaker. "As long as you give us what we want," he added in a sultry tone that sent a shiver down Bobby's spine.

"What-what do you want?" Bobby whispered, his gaze skittering between them.

"Your laptop," replied the first.

It almost drowned out the second guy's answer. "Your ass."

Bobby paled. "No," he denied.

"Aww, don't be that way, baby," the first guy said, leering. "We'll make it good for you."

Bobby didn't have anywhere to go when both guys moved in on him. He whimpered, cringing as the first guy's bad, beer-soaked breath wafted across his face. Crying out in dismay, Bobby shifted sideways when the second guy grabbed his belt. It didn't take a genius to realize what would come next.

He started to shake his head, and his body trembled violently. The first guy's fingers pinched his jaw and turned his head as he pressed his mouth over Bobby's and forced his tongue into his mouth.

Before Bobby could figure out how to get out of this, an inhuman roar echoed through the alley. Both men jerked, the first lifting his head though he kept his hands on Bobby's face. The second guy released his unbuckled belt and snarled, "What the fuck was that?"

"No fucking idea," the first man replied, his tone a cross between worried and angry, probably at the interruption.

"Why don't you pick on someone your own size?"

The question, spoken slowly, menacingly, in a deep gruff voice, actually vibrated Bobby's balls. That could be the only reason Bobby could think of that would explain why his dick started perking up under these circumstances. At least asshole mugger number one released his jaw and both stepped away from him to face the interloper.

Bobby knew he should take advantage of their distraction, so he sucked in a breath and sprinted toward the mouth of the alley. He didn't make it two steps before thug number two grabbed him and slammed him against a wall. Pain shot through his head as it scraped against the rough stone.

Another roar echoed through the alley. Instead of making his head ring, Bobby felt almost . . . well . . . reassured. He pressed a hand to his temple and felt the blood oozing from his skin. Instead of focusing on that, he couldn't help but notice the way the man who cast the massive shadow and spoke in the deep sexy voice slammed the head of one of the muggers against the wall.

He shouted a warning when he spotted the second man charge toward the shadow that signified his hero, a glimmer of moonlight glinting off the knife of a switchblade clutched in the attacker's hand.

The big shadow swept a long leg out and knocked the guy off his feet. The first mugger had regained his feet and charged. Bobby's hero swung out an arm and nailed the guy with his cloak. It must have been made of a stiff material, because the thug bounced backward into the wall. This time, his head hit it with a resounding crack and he slumped on the ground.

Bobby watched his helper's silhouette rise to his full height as he backhanded the second charging mugger. Like his buddy, when the man went down, he didn't get back up. Bobby's jaw dropped when his savior finally stood still and he could take in the guy's actual proportions. Sure, the shadows obscured quite a bit, but the man must have been at least seven feet tall, and his broad shoulders, holy shit!

"Are you all right?" the guy queried.

"Yeah," Bobby whispered, unable to stop his gaze from sweeping over the heavily cloaked, shadowed figure. "Thank you."

"Your laptop," the man said, kneeling on the ground and grasping a black, square object. "Here."

Instead of moving toward him, the man slid the bag across the concrete toward Bobby. His aim was true, and the bag stopped a foot in front him. "Thank you," he said again, grabbing it and pulling it close.

"You're welcome," came the guy's deep voice. "You can go. I'll call the police and deal with these thugs."

Bobby's fists tightened on the handle, but he didn't move from his spot. For some reason, he desperately wanted to see the face of his hero. He just knew it would be as sexy as his deep voice implied. Instead, he asked, "Is there something I can do to repay you for your kindness?"

For a long moment, the man remained quiet. Bobby almost didn't think he'd respond, but then the stranger said, "Have dinner with me."

He knew his brows lifted, and he couldn't keep in his surprised gasp. He licked his lips and struggled to formulate an answer. Would it be cheating to accept a thank-you dinner from a guy who saved him from . . . well, probably a mugging and rape?

Bobby decided Seth would probably see it that way. This was the perfect opportunity to move on. If this big man made his interest known, surely Seth would leave him alone, right?

"Never mind," the man said, refocusing Bobby's attention. The man moved, his shadow turning, drawing away.

"No, wait, please," Bobby cried, heading toward him.

ABOUT THE AUTHOR

Charlie started writing fantasy when she was eight, and after stumbling onto her first erotic romance at age nineteen, she realized her true calling. She now focuses on writing gay erotic romance, normally of the paranormal variety, with heroes of all kinds. With the help and support of her husband, Charlie finally fulfilled one of her life-long goals . . . move to acreage with her horses. You can often find her curled up with her laptop and a cup of tea or glass of wine, creating her next adventure. Charlie enjoys exploring the mountains of her new Oregon home on horseback, 4-wheeler, or motorcycle.

She can be reached at ch.richards2010@yahoo.com
Or visit her at www.charlie-richards.com

www.ingramcontent.com/pod-product-compliance
Lightning Source LLC
Chambersburg PA
CBHW070535130626
46555CB00003B/1432